HER SUBMISSION

THE DIRTIER DUET BOOK TWO
GABE'S STORY

NEW YORK TIMES BESTSELLING AUTHOR
LISA RENEE JONES

ISBN-13: 978-1091111523

Copyright © 2019 Julie Patra Publishing/Lisa Renee Jones

All rights reserved. No part of this publication may be reproduced, distributed, or transmitted in any form or by any means, including photocopying, recording, or other electronic or mechanical methods, without the prior written permission of the publisher, except in the case of brief quotations embodied in critical reviews and certain other noncommercial uses permitted by copyright law.

To obtain permission to excerpt portions of the text, please contact the author at lisareneejones.com.

All characters in this book are fiction and figments of the author's imagination.

www.lisareneejones.com

CHAPTER ONE

abbie

Dead.

I can barely process that word. Kenneth, a man I once called husband, is dead, no longer walking this earth.

Gabe's office starts to close in around me. This isn't happening. I can't breathe. I can't even process words to speak them.

"Abbie," Gabe says softly, his fingers flexing on my shoulders, his big body close, a hard, solid wall of support I need right now. "Talk to me," he orders, cupping my face and tilting my eyes to his. "Are you okay?"

"I'm—I'm in shock, I think." I swallow hard. "How? How did he die?"

"No word on how. The police haven't gone public yet."

Because it's murder, I think, because I can't bear to say this out loud.

"Wait? What? It's not public? How do you know before I know?"

"Someone who works for Jean Claude under my father called Reid."

"To tell him that Kenneth is dead," I say, still trying to process all of this.

"Yes. Kenneth is dead, Abbie."

Panic starts to rise inside me and I'm back to not being able to breathe. I did this. I made the call that did this and now, now I'm acting shocked. Like I didn't know what would happen if I made the call I made. Panic rises inside me. "I need to go. I need out of here."

I try to pull away from Gabe, but he catches my waist, holding me to him. "Why are you running?"

"I need air, Gabe. I need to breathe." Tears start to prickle my eyes.

"You were still in love with him," he accuses.

"What? No. God, no, but I didn't—this isn't how I thought it would end. I thought—I need to go, Gabe."

"You're crying. I mean, I get it. He was your husband, but fuck. I didn't think you still—"

"I'm not crying. I'm not. I—"

He swipes dampness from my cheeks. "You're crying, Abbie. Talk to me. I need to understand what you're feeling right now."

"I need to leave, Gabe."

"Oh no. You're not going anywhere without me. Not until we know what's going on. You're too connected to him."

I grab his lapels. "And he was murdered, right?"

"We don't know for sure yet."

"*For sure*? Was Reid told it was murder?"

"We don't know for sure."

"That's a yes. We *do know*. Why not just say that, Gabe? He *was murdered*. The police always look at the ex-spouse. They'll look at you, too, if you're close to me." And then they'll know what I did. Then he'll know. I shove at his chest. "Get back, Gabe. Let me go." I try to pull away again. He isn't having it, he still holds me firmly.

"Stop and listen to me, Abbie. Pushing me away does neither of us any good."

"No, you listen. He was coming at me, my mother, and most recently because of me, you, Gabe. We *are both* suspects. You know we are. That's how this works. You haven't known me long. Distance will protect you."

HER SUBMISSION

There's a knock on the door and by the time I've turned toward the sound, Reid's inside the office, shutting the door behind him. "I talked to Reese. He needs you both to come to him at the courthouse. He's in trial. He'll see you during his break."

"Reese?" I ask, looking between the two brothers. "As in your brother-in-law who just helped us at the shelter? The criminal attorney? We need Reese?"

"Just his name will give law enforcement pause," Reid replies. "He's that good. They'll step more cautiously where you two are concerned once he's formally named as your attorney."

"It's a precaution," Gabe interjects quickly. "Just a precaution."

"Because Kenneth was murdered," I say. "Say it, Gabe. He was murdered."

His lips thin. "Okay, Abbie. Yes. That's the information Reid was given. He was murdered."

And there it is. *He was murdered.* And I was involved. Oh God, I was involved. This is all exploding in my face, *what I did* is exploding in my face, and I can't let that catch Gabe and take him down with me. "If we need precautions," I say, "then you need to take a step back, from this and me." And knowing this stubborn man, won't listen, I turn a plea on Reid, appealing to a man I tried to hire for his cold-hearted reputation. "Protect your brother. I need out of this room and out of his life." I take a step toward the door.

Reid blocks my path. "What he needs," he says, his blue eyes hard. "Is what you need. To talk to Reese. You're already linked to my brother, but the good news here is that the list of people who hate your ex and might kill him is long."

"We're going to the courthouse," Gabe says, turning me to face him. "We're going to talk to Reese about what to do next. That conversation needs to include your mother at some point. You need to call her, warn her, and let her know that he's her attorney. Keep her silent until we can formally connect her with Reese."

"My mother," I whisper, my hand pressing to my suddenly churning belly. "I pulled my mother into this. We should have just sold the property."

"I'll be waiting on you outside," Reid says, the door opening and shutting behind me with his obvious departure.

"We *are fine*," Gabe insists. "And we'll know more soon. Reid called Walker Security. They're our guys for anything and everything. They're well-connected and experts in all forms of law enforcement and security. They're getting the inside scoop on this for us."

"How fast will they know?"

"They're rapid fire. Like I said, we'll know more soon."

He's going big on this. He's afraid. I'm afraid and I have reason to be. "This is why I kept trying to push you away. Kenneth was trouble. I knew he'd try to hurt you. I just— I'm so sorry that I pulled you into this."

"I'm not sorry, Abbie. This would have happened no matter my involvement with you or not. Now, you're not alone. Not now. Not ever again, unless you choose to be. And I won't let you make that choice until this is over." He strokes my cheek. "You're stuck with me, baby. Get used to it."

I don't argue. He won't let me and at this point, it probably really is too late for him to turn away. As Reid said. We're connected now, all of us, for the good, the bad, and the ugly, and I have a feeling this is going to get *really* ugly. "What now?"

"We leave. We meet with Reese. We let him guide us. Walker has a car waiting for us." He laces the fingers of one hand with mine and guides me toward the door, leading me to a meeting that he thinks will offer me some relief but he's wrong. I just keep thinking about that call I made. I did this. Now I have to decide what to admit.

LISA RENEE JONES

CHAPTER TWO

gabe

Reid is waiting on us just outside my door, the dodgeball game with the staff to get out of the office is unavoidable, but finally, we step onto the elevator with Abbie on one side of me and Reid on the other. I pull Abbie close by my side, under my arm, hating the fear this has created in her. I knew that could happen. I knew that if I went after her ex, she might feel some temporary pain, but not this. This was not the plan. I'm not a fool who dives into trouble and screams "look at me."

Reid punches the button for the lobby and we share a look: we need to talk. The two-minute-long conversation we'd managed before Abbie showed up in my office wasn't enough. But he damn sure came through for me. He's why we have an early heads up. He's the one who called Reese without me asking him to make the call. We have each other's backs and in our case with our father, that's our way of survival.

"Do I need to have my mother come back from the Hamptons?" Abbie says, obviously spending the ride down fretting. "Or is she safer there, out of the spotlight?"

"She needs to be here to talk to Reese and get any interviews over with," I say.

"We can have a chopper fly her back," Reid offers. "I'll make a call and arrange it before you contact her."

"Where's Carrie?" I ask, catching a flash of his new wedding ring. "Did your new wife actually let you come back to the states alone?"

"Not a chance in hell Carrie would let that happen," Reid replies. "She's at Cat's place picking up the furry family."

"And now I've ruined his honeymoon," Abbie says. "I'm starting things out with the family fabulously."

"My honeymoon wasn't ruined," Reid rebuts. "We had one hell of a time, but we were both ready to be back. This is nothing, Abbie. A blip on the radar, gone in a few days."

"A blip," I agree. "We're going to meet with Reese, offer up an alibi by way of the security footage from both my apartment and the house in the Hamptons, and then we'll go enjoy lunch somewhere."

"Or go to the police station because they haul us both in," she murmurs, the elevator dinging our arrival to the lobby.

I wrap my arm around her, and we follow Reid out of the car. "Just lunch," I promise. "Italian sounds good, don't you think?"

She doesn't reply and I leave it alone. I get it. Nothing I say is going to comfort her right now and why would it? A man she was married to is dead. Reese is the man to make her feel better this time. Not me.

For now, I concentrate on getting us there to make that happen. Once we're outside, I pause at the rear door of a hired SUV, my arm around Abbie beneath her coat, holding onto her the way I plan to keep holding onto her. "Let me talk to Reid for a few moments."

"About me. About what I got you into."

"You know what, baby? Tonight I'm going to punish you in all kinds of naughty ways for every time you tried to make yourself my enemy today." I kiss her. "We are not enemies. I just need a word with Reid. Okay?"

"Yes," she breathes out. "Yes. Sorry. I'm a bit paranoid right now."

"Understandable. I'll only be a moment."

"Should I call my mother?"

"Not yet. Let me find out if Walker has an update for us, and her, first." I soften my voice. "Kenneth is gone. That doesn't benefit you. Jean Claude still wants what he wants and that means your property. You had nothing to win by killing Kenneth and everything to lose."

"To lose? What did I have to lose besides a stalker?"

That stalker situation is a potential problem and motive, which is exactly why I leave it alone for now. "The police could assume that Kenneth might have had a soft spot in negotiations with you, even helped you out."

"We're talking about Kenneth, here. He helped no one but himself."

"But he was your ex. Jean Claude has no loyalty to you and no soft spot for anyone." I stroke her hair from her eyes. "Get warm in the vehicle. We'll be right there." I set her away from me and start to turn. She catches my arm.

"I hate that you're involved and yet so damn relieved that you're here."

The emotion in her voice undoes me. "I got you, Abbie, baby," I promise, kissing her again. "All the way. Every day." I turn her to the backseat, eager to just get this done and over with. "I'll be right there." Obedient for once, she does as I say and climbs inside.

I quickly shut the door behind her, my attention already turning to Reid, who motions me to the back of the SUV where he asks the same question he asked right before Abbie had walked in. "How much trouble is this for you and us?"

I scrub my jaw. "He threatened me and now he's dead, but the only person who heard that threat was Abbie."

"Threatened you how?"

"With a coded piece of my past better left in my past, that he wouldn't know about if dad hadn't told him."

"In other words, dad's really fucking involved in all of this."

"Is that a surprise?" I ask. "Isn't he behind most of the shit we deal with these days?"

"Was Abbie there during the exchange with Kenneth?"

"Yes and that was intentional. Dad knows this isn't something I want Abbie to hear from someone else."

Reid doesn't ask for details. He's focused on actions. "How did you handle the threat, Gabe? Because we both know you tried to talk me out of coming back. We both know you wanted me to stay away from this for a reason."

"I damn sure wasn't giving Kenneth the chance to ruin us. I started the process to destroy him, but there's no way that ties back to me or us. I made sure of it."

His cellphone rings and he grabs it from his pocket, eyes the number and then me. "Walker." He answers the call and when I would listen in, I hear the back door of the SUV open.

"Gabe!" Abbie calls out. "Gabe!"

At the urgency in her voice, I rotate to walk toward her, only to have her rush at me. "It's on the news," she says. "I just saw it on my phone. No details but his death is public now."

Reid rounds the vehicle and joins us. "I have the details. I just talked to Blake Walker. Kenneth took a bullet between the eyes. It was an assassination, a professional hit."

Abbie grabs my arms, twisting my jacket in her fingers. "That means your camera footage won't save you."

"She right," Reid agrees. "The police will be looking for the person, or persons, who hired the killer. And you'll both be on the suspect list. Blake is already working to pull together the electronic data to clear your names."

"Electronic data?" Abbie asks.

"Yes," Reid says. "Emails, phone records, and financial records for starters."

Abbie's knees go weak and I catch her waist, holding her up. "I need to talk to you alone," she whispers. "*Now*."

LISA RENEE JONES

CHAPTER THREE

gabe

Abbie's panic is palpable and with about ten alarms going off in my head, I pull her to the passenger door of the SUV, out of Reid's earshot. "Talk to me," I say, hands settling on her waist, just in case she decides that whatever this is, is yet another reason to bolt.

"That's just it," she says. "I can't. That's what I want to say to you. If Reese is going to represent me, I need to talk to him in private or he can't be my attorney."

"You have every right to speak to him alone, but I don't like how this vibes right now, Abbie. This is my brother-in-law, my pregnant sister's husband, you're about to have as your attorney. What am I pulling him into? What haven't you told me?"

"I didn't kill him, if that's what you think," she says. "But—it's complicated." She holds up a hand. "I can't talk about this. What you don't know, can't hurt you. If I tell you everything, and you're questioned or put under oath—"

"Hire me," I say, because I don't know what she did, but I need to know before we get to the courthouse. "If I'm one of your attorneys, what you tell me is privileged."

"You aren't my attorney, Gabe. We have no official contract."

I reach in my pocket, pull out my money clip, and hand her a dollar. "Pay me and tell me I'm hired."

"Gabe—"

"Do it, Abbie," I bite out, feeling the pressure of Reese's courtroom schedule.

"You're so damn stubborn," she hisses but she shoves the money in my hands. "You're hired."

"Tell me," I order, pocketing the dollar.

"I'm afraid I caused this."

"What does that mean?"

"I found some incriminating documents a few years back, proof that Kenneth stole from Jean Claude. When he came at you, I hit a limit. I didn't want you to suffer for me. I had Jean Claude's business card in my wallet. I thought if he went at Kenneth, broke off their financial arrangement even, that Kenneth would have his hands full. He'd back off. They'd leave us alone."

"You sent the documents to Jean Claude?"

"Yes," she says grimly. "I sent them. I told a brutal man that another man stole from him and someone ended up dead. Kenneth ended up dead. I caused this. Jean Claude—"

"Is responsible for whatever Jean Claude did. You didn't do this."

"We both know they will look at me and look hard." Her jaw clenches. "I kissed you and then dragged you right into hell. That's what this feels like."

"This isn't hell. This is you and me putting your hell behind us." Hell was where I was living before I ever found her, but I don't say that. I don't intend to ever tell her that story.

"Cat just texted me," Reid announces, rejoining us. "Reese is going to be another half hour but traffic is heavy. We need to get moving."

Abbie's cellphone rings. "That's going to be my mother," she says, reaching in the pocket of her jacket and grabbing her phone. "It's her," she says, glancing at the screen. "I'm taking it." She answers the line. "Mom," she greets, already walking away.

I let her go, turning to face Reid, giving him the full update.

"I have only one question for you," he says. "The only one that matters. The one I haven't directly asked you. If she didn't order the hit, who did? Did you?"

"I didn't order the fucking hit, Reid. And I can't believe you even asked me that."

"We both know why I did."

He's talking about my involvement in the little prick who stalked our sister a few months back ending up in the hospital. "I don't have time to go down this rabbit hole. You're no boy scout, Reid."

"I never pretended to be. That's where we differ. I'm an asshole who claims to be an asshole. You're Mr. Nice Guy with all your jokes and funny stuff, but we both know that you cut ten blades deep when someone crosses you."

"When someone tries to hurt someone I care about," I correct. "And don't expect me to apologize for that. I won't. I go after those who deserve it. I protect those who deserve it."

"Just make sure she deserves it," he warns. "You barely know her. She was married to a bastard of a man for a long time. Like minds attract."

"Don't be an asshole, Reid. She was afraid to leave him. Hell, she was afraid to get close to me because of him. Even her mother was afraid for her to get close to me."

"Maybe her mother was afraid she'd eat you alive."

"Careful, Reid," I warn. "If this was Carrie, how would you react to having her attacked?"

He arches a brow. "Is that how serious this is? You think she's your Carrie? Because I repeat, you just fucking met her."

"She's not going anywhere, Reid. You want to protect me, you protect her. If you can't do that, step away. Go the fuck back to Italy." I turn away, but he catches my arm.

I bite down and face him again. "What?"

"I'll fight for her. I just need you to answer one more question."

"You're out of questions."

"The one question left that matters to me. Do you trust her, and I mean, do you trust her *completely*?"

CHAPTER FOUR

gabe

Trust is not something I give easily and with good reason. I've been cut. I've been bruised, I've had my heart murdered and sewn it back together, with years of pain, in the process. So do I trust Abbie?

"Yes," I say, facing Reid fully again, letting him see how much I mean that declaration. "I trust her."

A flicker of surprise touches his expression. "Those are big words coming from you."

"She was honest with me," I add. "She told me what she did. She told me she went after her ex through Jean Claude."

"Because she had to," Reid says. "Because she's cornered. Why didn't she talk to you before she took action? She came to us, to me, to our firm, for help."

"Kenneth threatened me. She was afraid for me, and us."

"If there's anything you aren't telling me, if there's anything I need to know, speak it now."

"What don't you know? I'll tell you. Beyond reason and time, that woman matters to me. That's what you fucking *need to know.*"

He studies me for several expanding beats before he gives a sharp nod of his chin.

"I can't seem to get through to my mother," Abbie frets, stepping to my side.

"I thought you took her call?" I ask.

"I did," she confirms, "but the call dropped and I can't seem to get back to her now."

"Let's call her from the courthouse," I suggest. "We don't want to miss Reese's recess."

Her cellphone rings again and she glances at her caller ID. "It's her. I'll take it in the car." She answers the line. "Mom. Mom. Yes, I know. I'm fine, but I need you to come back here."

"Tell her to go to the airport," I say. "We'll have a chopper waiting for her." She nods and starts to turn away, headed for the backdoor. I catch her arm. "I need her to avoid the police until we get her prepped with Reese."

She covers the phone. "That's going to make her feel like there's a problem."

"Just being cautious, baby," I say. "We're all going to be questioned. That's expected. Prepare her but keep her calm."

Her expression tightens but she gives me a choppy nod.

"Abigail?" her mother says, her voice lifting through the line.

"Yes, mom," Abbie replies, returning her attention to the call.

I release her and she turns away while Reid steps close, huddling up with me. "I need to point out the obvious before Reese does: Abbie was married to a billionaire. She has to have the money to pay for a hit."

"She walked away with nothing but the shelter."

His brows lift. "Nothing?"

"I told you. She was afraid of him."

"Then go with that. You said Abbie and her mother were afraid of Kenneth. What would a mother do to protect her child?"

"You think my mother did this?"

At the sound of Abbie's voice, we both turn to look at her and her eyes burn into me.

"She didn't do this."

She tries to walk away. I pull her back to me, giving Reid my back. "No, I don't think your mother did this and as for Reid, better he asks the questions before the police, so we're ready for them."

Her lashes lower, her expression pained. "I hate this." She looks at me. "I hate this beyond words. I hated him beyond words. I can't lie about that and be believable."

"And yet you were married to him for five years," I say, playing devil's advocate.

Her eyes flash angrily. "Did you really just say that me?"

"Reid just said it to me. Reese will say it as well."

"You know why." She cuts her stare. "It's complicated."

I catch her chin and turn her gaze to mine. "I know why. You were afraid of him but fear can be a motive. That's going to come up. You're going to have to talk to Reese about it. You're going to have to talk to the police about it. And so is your mother."

"I wish my mother could just be left out of this."

"How was she on the phone? Where is she?"

"Worried but calm. She's headed to the airport."

Calm. I'm not sure that's what I expected but she's a vet who deals with critical emergencies. Calm might be her panic but I don't comment. I open the back door of the SUV and urge Abbie forward. "Let's get this over with."

She nods and climbs into the vehicle. I join her, tension radiating between us that came from nowhere and yet everywhere. I reject what can only hurt us, pulling her close, silently telling her that I'm here. I'm not going anywhere. Reid climbs into the front passenger seat and the driver pulls us onto the road.

None of us speak.

But without question, we're all thinking about the same thing: murder.

The ride is short, and not more than fifteen minutes later, we're inside a large room, sitting at a conference table, me beside Abbie, Reid at the end of the table. We've barely sat down when Cat walks in, her hand on her growing belly, her dress a blue satin that clings to her body and highlights her pregnancy.

"My God," she declares dramatically shutting the door, blowing a long strand of blonde hair from her eyes. "What happened?" She looks at me, sizes me up, and with one glance warns me what's to come. She's going on the attack, and already she's refocused on Abbie. *"What* happened, Abbie?"

And just like that, in two words and her name, Cat's opened the door for a confession. To protect me. To protect her husband before he represents Abbie. To protect Abbie when she talks to the police, already seasoned from the internal attacks.

"Apparently murder," Abbie whispers, cutting her stare, emotion bleeding from her, crashing into me and I try not to let that affect me. Of course, she's emotional. She was married to the man. She's scared. It doesn't mean she loved him.

"And I hated him," she adds, and as if she spoke those words for me, to me, her eyes meet mine. "I hate him," she repeats, her gaze shifting back to Cat. "How can I say that and not end up looking guilty? I didn't kill him, Cat."

There is so damn much anguish in her voice that Cat reacts, her expression softening from accusation to understanding. "Oh, honey," she says, rushing forward to claim a seat at the table across from us. "Lot's of people hate their ex-husbands. That doesn't mean they kill them."

"But my ex really is dead," Abbie argues. "I'm not most people."

The door opens on that comment and Reese appears, dressed in an expensive three-piece suit, he radiates this kind of warrior arrogance that dominates this room and any courtroom he enters. He's confident. He's in charge. He's all business as he sets out to do what I know he does with all prospective clients before he offers comfort: he decides if he'll represent them. He tests them. He puts them on the spot. And I know that's what's about to happen. He sits down in front of Abbie, looks her in the eyes, and asks, "This was a contract killing, I'm told."

"Yes," Abbie says. "I was told the same."

Reese leans in a little closer to her, lowers his voice, as if he's talking to just Abbie, and no one else. "Did you want your ex-husband dead, Abbie?"

LISA RENEE JONES

CHAPTER FIVE

abbie

Did I want my ex dead?

That question hangs in the air between myself and Reese while the entire room waits for my answer.

"No," I say finally, too many seconds later. "I didn't want him dead. I have never wished anyone dead. Not even him."

Reese doesn't immediately reply. He's intimidating, his eyes probing and intense. My nerves bristle and I grip Gabe's hand where it rests on my knee under the table.

"It took you a long time to answer that question," Reese says, leaning in closer.

"You didn't ask if I killed Kenneth or even if I hired someone to kill him," I say. "You asked if I ever wanted him dead. If you'd have asked me those questions, my reply would have been fast. No, I didn't kill him. No, I didn't hire someone to kill him. But as to the question, did I ever want him dead? I hated him enough to need to consider my reply. I wanted to be honest."

Reese arches a brow. "Were you?"

"Yes."

"Why did you hate him?" Reese asks.

Why?

One word manages to be such a complicated, emotional, and personal question. A question that cuts and digs and bites. A question that exposes a part of me that I don't even want to know as me. A part of me that was weak, so very weak. I never want to be that weak again.

I look down, aware of the audience, uncomfortable with them. Uncomfortable with this answer reflecting my life.

"Leave us alone," Reese orders the room.

"No," I say quickly, meeting his stare. "You're going to tell Cat and I'm going to tell Gabe and one or all of you will tell Reid. They might as well stay."

"As your legal counsel," Reese replies, "should I become your legal counsel, I can assure you privacy, even with them."

"But what does that achieve?" I challenge. "These people are all protecting me. They deserve to know who I am." I don't give him time to argue. "Kenneth threatened me often." I glance at Gabe. "You know that, at least to some degree. You saw—"

"Yes," Gabe confirms. "I saw."

"Expand on the word threatened for me," Reese urges. "How did he threaten you?"

"Words mostly," I say and because I can't choke the rest of the sentence out while looking at Gabe, I look at Reese and add, "but he could be physically abusive as well."

Gabe pulls me around to him again. "That bastard hit you?"

I swallow hard. "Yes, Gabe. He hit me. He hit me and I know staying with him despite that was foolish but it was all about my mother. I had to protect my mother. I know that seems weak but—"

"Weak?" Gabe demands. "You think I think you're weak? You *are not* weak. You weren't weak by staying and you don't need to defend yourself in this room or to me. He was the asshole. He was the abuser."

Emotion wells in my chest and clogs my throat. "I should have found a way out."

"You did," Gabe says. "You got out."

"Gabe's right on all points," Reese states. "You don't need to defend yourself with us." He waits for me to look at him and then adds, "Unfortunately, abuse does provide the police with a motive for you to kill Kenneth."

"I didn't kill him," I bite out vehemently. "I didn't do this. I didn't hire someone to do this."

"Relax baby," Gabe says, catching my hand. "He's just stating facts."

"I believe you," Reese replies. "Gabe's right again. This is about facts and strategy. We'll decide what you need to share and with who when we know more about the murder."

"Then you'll represent me?" I ask.

"Yes," Reese says. "I will. I believe you're innocent and from what I've been told by Reid and Walker Security, there were plenty of people who wanted your ex dead. But I need to ask a direct question and get an honest answer. You said you were protecting your mother. Explain that."

"He threatened to hurt her if I left."

"And yet you left."

"Yes, well eventually he cared more for his other women, and less about me. It was like the bars came off the windows. He lost interest in me. I think he had a real thing for one of them. He asked for a divorce." I give a choked laugh. "It was the best day of my life to this point."

"*He* asked for the divorce?" Reid asks, looking confused, his gaze shooting to Gabe's, before returning to mine. "Why didn't you ask for a fair settlement?"

"He told me if I did, he'd punish me in creative ways I couldn't even begin to imagine. I couldn't believe he allowed me to keep the shelter but that felt safe. How could that possibly backfire on me? And yet, it did."

"Okay, Abbie," Reese says. "I think, for now, we're close to wrapping up."

Abbie. They all call me Abbie. Because of Gabe. Because he's shaping my life in ways I don't yet understand but I want to. I so want to. "Help Gabe stay out of this, Reese. Please. Put him first. He's what matters to me."

"I'm going to help you both," he replies. "If I'm even needed. If we're lucky this doesn't go beyond some basic questioning. They may have their man. I know only what you know," he says. "And that's not much, certainly nothing official." He pauses a split second. "I'll make a preemptive call on my way back into court, but if you're contacted by the police, tell them I'm your attorney and that you're dating my brother-in-law. That lets them know I won't let you talk and that I'm prone to being extra cautious on this one."

"That's great," I say. "Thank you."

"I'll let them know that I'm representing your mother as well, for the moment," he continues. "I need to meet her before I'll say that goes beyond initial law enforcement contact. Fair enough?"

"Yes," I say, relieved. "Thank you."

"No thanks needed," Reese assures me. "Now. Aside from me talking to Gabe, which I can do later tonight, is there anything else I need to cover with you, Abbie?"

"Yes actually," I say. "There's something you need to know before you make a call on my behalf."

Reese laces his fingers in front of him, settling in for more. "I'm all ears."

But so are Cat and Reid. I glance at Gabe and he nods. "Tell him. Reid knows. Cat is under a confidentiality clause with Reese's firm."

Tell his siblings that I all but killed my ex? Of course. Why not let them hate me right out of the gate? "My ex was threatening Gabe. He was threatening my mother. Bottom line, I not only told Jean Claude Laurette that my ex stole from him, but I gave him proof by email. I knew Jean Claude was a dangerous man but I believed he'd fire him not kill him."

"Telling Jean Claude about your ex stealing from him is not the same as contracting someone to kill him," Reese assures me. "You're fine." He winks. "You have me." He looks at Gabe, and almost nonchalantly, says. "Did you kill him?"

"No," Gabe states.

"Did you hire someone to kill him?"

"No," Gabe says again.

"Do you know who did?"

"No," Gabe replies. "But if I did, I'd send them flowers and chocolate. He was a snake, as is Jean Claude."

"A snake you and Reid worked for," Reese counters.

"I worked for him," Reid states. "Gabe wasn't in that circle. It was me and my father."

Gabe looks at Cat. "He's involved, Cat."

Cat frowns. "Who?"

"Dad. He's doing legal work for Jean Claude again now that he left the firm and Jean Claude had investments with Abbie's ex."

"Oh God," she whispers, eyeing Reese. "What if he did this to pin it on Gabe and Reid? As payback for pushing him out of the firm?"

"Your father's a dick, baby," Reese says. "But that hurts his legacy."

"He's already lost his legacy," Cat argues. "A trapped animal in a corner shows his teeth."

"You underestimate our teeth, sister," Reid assures her. "And we don't even have to be angry to show them."

Someone opens the door. "We need you, Reese."

"On my way," Reese calls over his shoulder, before looking at me. "I need to speak to your mother."

"We're flying her in from the Hamptons," Gabe supplies.

"Call Cat when she arrives," Reese instructs. "She'll communicate with me."

Gabe nods at Reese and Cat pats the table in front of me. "Be strong. This will all work out." She's sweet and kind, her support appreciated but I don't miss the way her voice is now a different octave, defeat just below the surface. Her father's involvement has changed this for her. She's worried and I'm not sure what to make of just how worried.

She and Reese stand, followed by Reid, and in a splatter of fast activity, Gabe and I are left to watch the door seal us inside the room alone, every mistake I've made since meeting Gabe tormenting me with its closure; the only kind of closure we have right now. Kenneth is the only one who has closure. The kind you don't come back from.

CHAPTER SIX

abbie

Hand in hand, Gabe and I follow the rest of the group, stepping out into the courtroom hallway where Cat is awaiting us. "Why don't you go to our place? There's no chance you'll get sideswiped that way. All the reporters stalking Reese are here right now." She looks at me. "Have your mother come to us, too. Then Reese can meet with her as soon as he's free."

"I have a dog now," Gabe says. "We need to get home."

"Bring him with you," Cat offers. "We love furbabies. We babysat Reid and Carrie's cat and dog while they were gone."

"What if my dog eats their cat?" Gabe challenges and despite all of this, I laugh.

"He named him Dexter," I explain, "and he did so because, despite all his friendliness, Gabe is certain that he's a killer."

Cat gives her brother a dubious look. "I'm certain that comes from a deep-rooted distrust of pretty much the entire world. Bring Dexter for a playdate. It sounds fun, and I think the baby wants pizza so we'll order pizza." She places her hand on her belly, considers a moment and then confirms. "Yes. Pizza. Non-negotiable."

I laugh but it comes out choked, my emotions masked but not buried. "Thanks, Cat, for everything. You two—or—" I glance at her belly, "three, have been nothing but wonderful to me, and even my mother. I know it's about protecting Gabe, but you've made me feel like an old friend."

"A new friend," she says. "You're one of us now and our clan protects our own, except for the father who would eat his own children." She hugs me I suspect to hide the emotions radiating in those words. "You're good for him," she whispers next to my ear. "You just don't know it yet." She releases me, and as she hugs Gabe, I'm quaking inside.

I'm good for him.

I want to be, but she's right. I really don't know it right now. Cat hurries back to court while Reid joins us. "Party at Cat's house. I heard." He eyes Gabe. "We need a minute."

"Because you want to talk about me and you can't when I'm with you?" I ask, because he couldn't get more obvious.

Reid's eyes dance with unfettered amusement. "You have a mouth on you, don't you?"

"Yes," Gabe says. "She does." He steps into me and cups my face. "Use it to get all of my secrets later when we're alone." My cheeks heat with the comment that Reid has to have heard, but Gabe is already kissing me. "Give me two minutes, baby." He releases me and walks away with his brother, that endearment of "baby" doing funny things to my belly.

I turn away from the two brothers, and stare down the long hallway, watching people hurry past, headed toward the courtrooms that hold destinies for both those who are on trial and those affected by the trial. I feel as if this is where I'm going to end up, with Reese defending me. I just have to make sure Gabe and my mother don't end up here, too.

"Ready, baby?" Gabe asks, sliding his arm around my shoulders and setting us in motion.

"What was that, Gabe?"

"Reid's going to take Dexter out. I told him to leave him at home. It might be too much for him to come with us. And

I don't want to take any chances of us getting cornered before we can get a game plan going with your mother."

"You're that worried?"

"Yes. Dexter is a killer."

"*Gabe,*" I say. "You know what I'm talking about."

"I like to do things on my terms," he says. "And that means the police get us when we know why they want us. When we have details and a plan."

"Can't Reid just call Jean Claude?"

"They parted on bad terms."

"Can you call your father?"

"He's the enemy." He turns us right down the hallway leading toward the side door. "We can't trust a word he says."

I don't have a father that I can call a father, not really, and he was really horrible to me and my mom, but to distrust him the way Gabe does his father—that's got to hurt. That's got to mess with you and I think of Cat's comment about trust. Gabe doesn't trust. I'm just thankful that I told him what I did. I wouldn't want to hide anything from him. Not with this history that I have a feeling runs much deeper than his father. It's about why he ensured he can't have babies. It's about that KM threat my ex threw out at him that he didn't talk to Reese about. He's going to have to talk to him. The thing is, will he talk to me? Will he trust me?

Maybe.

Eventually.

Not now.

We exit the courthouse with that thought on my mind, that certainty: no, he will not trust me. Not yet. I just have to understand that we're new. He's all in with me. I feel that, but emotional layers are created over years and years, over a lifetime. I can't expect full exposure now. I haven't even given him full exposure. I don't have secrets, but as we settle into the backseat of the SUV, and he pulls me close, I think of some of the things I endured with my ex. These things aren't easy to talk about. They aren't things I even think about. I'm a robot in some ways where my ex is concerned. That was survival. But what, I wonder, made a vasectomy survival for Gabe?

I lean into him, closer now and some part of me wants to hide in the shelter of his body. He's going to ask questions. He's going to push for more of my past, and if I really want him to share his, I'm going to have to share mine. Gabe must read my mind because he turns to me, cups my face, and strokes my cheek. "You were brave. You *are* brave. So fucking brave."

I don't know if he means with Reese and his family, or with my ex. It doesn't matter. I reject this description of me vehemently. "No. I'm not brave. I was not brave. I was a coward. You don't—"

He kisses me, a tender kiss, tongue stroking deep but slow, and when he pulls back he says, "I do. I know. More than you think I know." He runs his thumb over my lips and then settles into his seat.

I'm quaking inside again, but I'm warm in ways I didn't think I could ever feel warm again. It seems that since my ex, I've lived with ice inside, with a chill that would never heat, a part of me always a wrong move away from shattering.

Gabe knows more than I think he knows. He's said that kind of thing to me before. I'm not sure what he means. I just know that I'm remarkably at peace with those words, as if he's declared his soul knows my soul, his damage understands my damage. And maybe it does. Maybe he does. I just hope it's enough to get us through it all.

A few minutes later, we enter Cat and Reese's apartment building, and I'm now hyperaware of all the doors I opened, all the questions I invited when I talked about my past with Kenneth. Now, Gabe will ask questions and I decide on the elevator ride that I will give him answers without demanding he do the same for me. He's not ready for that and, I have to take risks with this man. Lord knows he's taken them with me by staying in this, by standing by me. I have to give trust to get trust, I decide, but the thing about trust is that it's fragile in its infancy. Trust is about being vulnerable and when you're vulnerable, you shatter easily. And what if you shatter into too many pieces? What if you can't pull yourself back together? What if you let the person destroy you?

LISA RENEE JONES

CHAPTER SEVEN

abbie

The minute we're inside his sister's apartment I know the questions will follow. Anticipation, dread, worry—these things knot in my belly, have burned through me with every step down the hallway leading to the apartment door. Now, waiting for Gabe to deal with security and then eventually unlock the door, my stomach is in knots and it's not like I'm not willing to share details with Gabe. This man has quickly found his way into my life where I want him to stay. He's helped me. He's involved himself in things that will cause him hell I don't want him to live. He deserves whatever answers he wants from me. It's just hard to talk about some of the things this conversation will expose.

He shoves open the door and when I would enter, he grabs me and kisses me. "Easy, baby. You're throwing off nerves and I don't know why. It's me. Just me. You know me now."

"Not as well as I want to know you, Gabe."

"And I want to know you, all of you, Abbie, but I get the idea that you think that's going to change?"

"I'm just—I'm feeling a little exposed, for a lack of a better word, right now."

He caresses my cheek. "Don't. Whatever you think I see when I look at you, you must not see what I see. When I think of what you went through—"

"You think weak and stupid?" I challenge, my heart lurching.

"I see nothing but strong and brave when I look at you, Abbie. Go inside. Let's talk. Let's kiss. Let's get past this." He strokes my bottom lip, heat waving off of him, crashing into me. "We definitely need to go inside." He turns me to face the door and smacks my backside playfully.

I yelp at the unexpected palm, laughing the way only Gabe could make me laugh right now, stepping into the apartment foyer as I do. That's when I laugh all over as I'm accosted by a Golden Retriever with a ball. Smiling broadly, I go down on my knee in front of the pup when a pretty brunette appears in the hall.

"I see you've met Nikki," she says. "Our kitty Kesha is hiding somewhere so don't let her scare you if she pounces." She smiles. "And I'm Carrie."

I pop to my feet. "Reid's wife, right?"

Gabe steps to my side and gives Nikki a pat. "Hi there, Nikki. Hey there, Carrie." He calls out, "Hi Kesha!" He eyes Carrie. "Hiding again?"

"Always," Carrie assures him, giving me a friendly look Gabe latches onto.

"This is Abbie," he announces.

"Nice to meet you, Abbie," Carrie says, "And yes to your prior question, I'm Reid's wife and that's still so new that it's crazy to say out loud."

So new they were literally just married and guilt stabs at me. "I hate you came back from your honeymoon early. I feel like it's my fault."

She waves that off. "Nonsense. We were both eager and ready to get home." She eyes Gabe. "Reid ran to your place to check on Dexter, but you know that. I can't believe you have a dog."

"That I blame on Abbie. She and her mother run a shelter and one thing led to another."

"One thing led to a lot of things," I say, looking at him. "Not all as good as Dexter."

"On that note," Gabe says. "We all need a drink."

"I made coffee," Carrie says. "Anyone want to join me?"

"Coffee sounds almost as good as whiskey," Gabe says. "Coffee with whiskey though, even better."

Carrie hurries down the hallway with Nikki on her heels and while Gabe and I remove our coats, Gabe leans in close to whisper, "Something tells me it's going to be a while before I get to kiss you the way I want to kiss you."

The way I want *him* to kiss *me*, but I also want this nightmare to be over with and with him feeling none of the aftermath. Carrie is Reid's wife. Reid is well-connected to the people who started all of this: the Maxwell father and Jean Claude. I want to know Carrie's take on all of this.

Gabe leads me down the hallway to join Carrie in a stunning large box-shaped kitchen with shiny tiles and stainless steel. Carrie settles at the island with a piping-hot cup of coffee, and the pooch at her feet.

Gabe leads me to the pot and the ease at which he opens cabinets and provides coffee supplies for us both tells me that he's comfortable in his sister's home. I like this about him, the bond he shares with siblings, that's enviable, even if it bares open the hole that is family in my life.

"So," Carrie says, as we join her, sitting across from her. "It sounds like things got interesting while we were traveling." Her hand covers mine on the island. "How are you?"

My chest pinches. These people, all of Gabe's people, settle into that open hole, as if they belong there, as if we're meant to be there.

"Scared," I admit. "I'm scared. I know I'm supposed to be sad, but I'm not, and I don't know how I talk to the police and not seem guilty because of that fact." I hear the lift to my voice, and I feel, oh how I feel, the hysteria that just this easily, with one little question, starts to bubble in my chest.

Gabe's hand comes down on my arm and I can't explain how, but he tamps down that hysteria. He calms me. He makes me feel safe. I trust this man when I didn't think I could trust again and it kills me to know that I'm going to end up burning him because I didn't walk away while I still could have. Because I was with him when this happened.

"I need some air," I say, scooting off the seat too quickly and losing my balance, but I find my footing and head toward I don't know what. I step into a hallway, aimlessly turning to my right.

Thankfully this path leads to a living area framed by floor-to-ceiling windows, as well as a sliding door leading to a balcony. I head for that door and in a rush of movement, I'm outside, cold air rushing over me, but I don't care. A motion detector trips lights and I hug myself, rushing to a railing with a city view that displays miles of city skyline, the city bursting with life. I imagine all the people down there, bustling about, rushing to and from, living life, the way I just want to get on with living life. I've tried. I've tried for years but Kenneth was never going to let that happen though. He's proven that in life and death.

The door opens behind me and I don't need to turn to know who is with me. I can feel Gabe join me. His energy. His strength. The charge between us that is ever-present. I feel him. I have never felt any man like I do this one. I revel in that sensation. It gives me life. He makes me feel alive. And then he's there, with me, stepping behind me, ever the gentleman, as he settles a blanket around my shoulders. "It's cold out here, baby. There are some warm, private spots in the apartment."

"I like the cold." I turn to him. "And the blanket. You're always taking care of me."

"Is that a bad thing?" he asks, reading the million layers to my emotions, even when I don't realize they're there, between us, owning their own little place, even when I think they don't.

"I swore I'd take care of myself from now on."

He grabs the edges of the blanket and walks me to him. "But now you don't have to take care of yourself. You have me. You don't fully know that yet, but you will. You will know you have me."

"I know right now that I have you."

"Right now," he repeats. "Meaning soon I'll be gone."

"Kenneth will drive you away. You just don't know it yet."

"No one, dead or alive, will drive me away," he replies. "Try to relax. This will be over quickly. I know how Jean Claude and my father work. All of this is too close to them. They'll make it go away."

"By pinning it on us?"

"We're a complicated layer of shit on their show. We aren't how this ends for them."

He's confident. I see that in his face. I see more there, too. "What do you know that I don't know?"

LISA RENEE JONES

CHAPTER EIGHT

gabe

What doesn't she know?

Much.

There is much she doesn't know and she won't know. Ever.

That question hangs in the cold night air that shifts with a gust of wind. Abbie shivers and I let go of the blanket that I've wrapped around her. "I'll turn on the fireplace." I don't wait for her reply. I walk to the wall by the sliding door and flip on the outdoor fireplace I should've turned on when I exited in the first place.

Abbie follows me, steps to me again in front of the fireplace. "What don't I know Gabe?" Her eyes narrow on me. "Oh God. Tell me you didn't—"

"I didn't what, Abbie?"

"Hire the assassin. You didn't, right?"

That question punches me in the chest. "I answered that question for Reese."

"Answer it for me. Just me. Did you have Kenneth killed?"

Did I have her ex-husband killed?

And there it is. A question I created by making her prior question of "what don't I know" become more complicated than it had to be, by making it about everything, not one thing. Not one fucking thing, as it was intended.

"No. I didn't hire a hitman to kill your ex-husband and can I say, just using the word 'husband' where you're concerned pisses me the fuck off. After knowing you, and knowing him, I don't understand how you ended up with him."

Her eyes widen and she tries to turn away. "Fuck," I murmur, and catch her arm, pulling her back to me. "That wasn't about you."

"It sounded like it was about me." She hangs onto the blanket but doesn't touch me. "It sounded judgmental and pompous and—"

"All of those things. Yes. But it wasn't about you." My jaw sets hard and I look at the flames now flickering in the fireplace, old demons clawing at me, and it's pissing me off. The past doesn't get to have that kind of control over me. I step closer to Abbie. "Look, I'm all too aware of the fact that I just responded to you based on my past, not the present. And *you're* the present. *My* present."

"You do know that I have plenty of reasons to judge you by my past, right? My very recent, extremely raw past."

"No," I say rejecting that idea, but choosing my words cautiously. "You don't. I haven't given you any reason to believe that I'm going to let you down the way your ex let you down."

"And I have you?" she demands. "Because that's what this is about, right? An ex?" She tilts her head. "Is KM an ex?"

It's an inevitable question I don't intend to answer. "What this is," I say, directing us away from KM, making this about Abbie, which is safer than making it about me, "is me asking what the police will ask. How did someone like you end up with that asshole?"

"I didn't choose to be with an asshole. He didn't seem like an asshole at the time."

"How did you meet him?"

"A charity event, which obviously contributed to me feeling like he was a good guy. He donated big that night. He asked me to dinner. He wined and dined me."

"And you fell in love." The idea grinds through me with ridiculous amounts of jealousy. I didn't know her then.

"I think it was more infatuation," she replies. "He seemed to have the world in his hands and it was powerful. It was interesting. And yet, he seemed so kind."

"When did you discover the real man?"

"Six months after I married him, he changed. Or rather, he showed his true colors."

"Why did he go to that kind of effort to convince you that he was what he wasn't?"

She laughs bitterly. "Right. Because he couldn't possibly have been in love with me?"

I scrub my jaw and drag her to me. "You could make any man fall in love with you, Abbie," I say, aware that it's exposing me. That I'm standing on a limb for this woman, waiting for it to break. "Anyone human, that is," I add. "He wasn't human, any more than my father is human. What did he want from you?"

"He was going to run for office. I think he thought me and my charity work looked good by his side." Her voice cracks. "I don't think he ever loved me."

But I could, I think. *Holy hell,* I could.

"Why didn't he run for office?"

"A financial scandal. I don't know much about it."

A reason for someone to kill him. "Tell the police. Tell Reese."

"Yes. Of course. I will." She grabs my shirt, letting the blanket fall. "You aren't going to tell me about KM, are you?"

Those demons claw at me again, and again. And fucking again. They will always claw at me. "KM was a business associate who tried to fuck me," I say, and it's not a lie.

Kendall and I worked together. We also fucked. And she tried to fuck me in a way few could imagine possible.

"And you won?"

"No. No, I didn't win, which is exactly why my father likes to taunt me with it."

She studies me a moment, intelligent eyes, sizing me up and well. "None of that is a real answer."

"It's the truth."

"It's half-truths," she accuses.

My jaw clenches. "Everything I said was true."

"Sorry," she says. "Bad wording. I meant it's half the story." Her hand goes to my face. "Don't talk about it. I get it. Some things are difficult. Some things cut to relive."

"You mean his abuse," I say, and it's not a question. "Your abuse."

"It's not the abuse that gets me. It's the way I handled it. It's the way I became his puppet. Maybe had I gotten out sooner, it wouldn't have gotten so hard to get out. Once we owned that shelter, once my mother and all the animals were depending on it, I felt trapped. He'd threaten her and the shelter."

"And yet he let you keep it."

"I think in the end, he was just damn glad to keep his money. That's why him wanting the shelter makes no sense. Maybe it was vindictive. Maybe it's over, but that is going to look like a motive."

"We'll know soon," I say. "If Jean Claude wants the property, he'll come at you right away. There will be no mourning process. He doesn't have a heart."

"And I told him about my ex stealing from him. He had to have killed him."

This is the moment when I could tell her what I did. When I could give her the relief of knowing that I may well have caused Kenneth's death, but I believe it would be more cold comfort. She'd blame herself for my actions. Because that's who she is. She takes things on herself. She blames herself while I feel no guilt over assholes who get what they deserve. A part of me my clients appreciate, but Abbie will not.

I pull her flush against me, my body hard, hers soft. I want her. I think I might even need her. That means that while I won't lie to her, I have to keep secrets. I have to keep my past, my past. I have to keep what I did to protect her buried. And I will. She will never know what I did. She will never know about KM.

LISA RENEE JONES

CHAPTER NINE

gabe

The sliding glass door opens and Carrie pokes her head out. "We're about to have a houseful. Reid, Reese, and Cat are all about to arrive. And FYI, the prosecution asked for an early recess, but apparently, Reese did talk to law enforcement."

"And?" Abbie asks, pulling away from me to face Carrie.

"Not much," Carrie says, shivering. "You have to come inside to talk to me. I can't take the cold. Sorry." Carrie disappears inside.

Abbie tries to rush toward her. I catch her arm and turn her back to me. "Easy, baby. Everything is going to be fine. I promise you."

"You can't make that promise. Don't make a promise you can't keep."

There's a hint of agitation with that reprimand that I don't miss. She's been burned. She's been made promises her ex didn't keep. Maybe it even ties back to her MIA father. People have let her down. I won't.

"I don't make promises that I can't keep. We're going to be fine. Separately and together. You'll see. And you'll also see that I'm a man of my word, Abbie."

She breathes out. "I'm sorry. You've given me every reason to trust you, Gabe, but people say things to comfort others and I don't want everyone to keep telling me that it's going to be okay. I hate fluff comfort. Words don't fix problems."

"No," I say, aware that while she might not realize it, she's allowing me to see her fears, to understand them, and that's a massive step between us I won't allow her to regret. "I'm not using words to comfort you. I'm using knowledge and trust. Reese's knowledge and my trust in his skills. I want you to remember that as we move forward."

I turn us toward the door and this time she catches my arm. "I'm sorry."

"What are you sorry for?"

"I'm sorry that I judged you by everyone before you when we just talked about not letting our pasts dictate our present together."

I drag her to me and kiss her. "Show me later when we're finally alone."

"I will," she promises, her lips curving. "And I'll be thinking of all the ways I can do that between now and then."

"Now you're just teasing me."

"Yes," she says. "I am." Her voice softens. "And I like it."

The way she says those final words, all soft and sweet, it's clear she's not talking about sex. She's talking about us, about this, whatever is happening between us. "As do I," I whisper, my fingers caressing her cheek, goosebumps lifting on her skin, a shiver following.

"Let's get you inside and warm," I say leading her back into the house where we join Carrie in the kitchen.

"Any other updates?" Abbie asks, settling on a barstool while I sit down on the one next to her and across from Carrie.

"The police want to question you both," Carrie says. "Reese is coordinating his court schedule with them but I think it's going to be a few days out."

"An eternity to worry about how this is going to turn out," Abbie whispers, staring down at her cold cup of coffee. "I can't take it."

I grab her cup, drawing her attention to mine. "A day gives them time to find answers and decide they don't need us." I sip from the mug. "And that's cold."

Carrie stands and takes it from me. "Let me warm that up for you." The doorbell rings.

"That must be Reid," Carrie says, setting the cup right back down in front of me. "That door automatically locks with some new security system Reese and Cat installed. I don't think he has the code to get in yet."

Wanting another chat with Reid alone, I push to my feet. "I'll get it." I wink at Abbie. "I love to see my cold-hearted bastard of a brother greet his dog with baby voices." I don't give her time to question my intentions, hurrying out of the room.

Once I'm at the door, I confirm it's Reid and let the bastard in and sure enough, he does the baby voices as he greets Nikki. It's like a show you never thought you'd see and get to see it on repeat. "Dexter likes me," he says, tossing Nikki's ball and watching her disappear into the other room. "I think he needs to move in with us."

"Forget it, man. Dexter would rip your throat out if he got the chance," I promise. "I've seen what you haven't."

Reid lowers his voice. "So he's hiding behind the nice guy routine? Sounds familiar."

I grimace. "You got something to say, say it."

"You don't have to play nice with me. I don't have to play nice with you. If you're getting serious about Abbie, you have to be honest with her. Are you prepared to do that?"

"Fuck man. You have to go there today?"

"Yeah, I do. The demon door has to be opened."

"Shit man, you think I need to go commando with her before I've even asked her to move in with me? What the fuck, Reid?"

"You know that's not what I'm saying, but I talked to Carrie. She likes Abbie. She loves you. She says that Abbie is good for you if you don't destroy her before she does her good mojo on you."

"Carrie doesn't know me."

"She knows more than you think she knows. I sure as fuck do."

"Stop making me the devil that ripped the panties off a fucking angel that I'm about to drag to hell."

"We both know this thing with her husband—"

"Ex-fucking-husband."

"Ex-fucking-husband," he amends, "is going to get dirty. We both know you already got dirty. She's going to find out."

"There's nothing to find out," I say. "Not a damn thing."

"You don't get to be the old you with her if you want her to be a significant part of your life."

She's already significant, I think, but I stay on point with what matters in this conversation. "What is your point, brother asshole?"

"We are our father's sons," Reid says. "We can go dark. You've gone dark before and so have I. We both know you went dark to protect Cat from that stalker."

"This again?"

"Yes. This again."

"I handled what you wouldn't and now you're flipping it on me?"

"You protected our sister at all costs. All I'm saying is that Carrie changed me and how I handle myself but I had to be willing. If you aren't willing to change, then you need to walk away from Abbie."

HER SUBMISSION

I look up to find Abbie standing in the hallway, staring at us.

LISA RENEE JONES

CHAPTER TEN

gabe

Abbie stands there and says nothing. She just stares at me and Reid with those big green eyes of hers, red curls teasing the delicate features of her lovely face. She doesn't question me or him. She doesn't demand answers. She doesn't turn and run and thank fuck for that. I need this woman. In every way, in every part of me, I need this woman.

I cross the foyer, close what has become the unbearable space between me and her, stopping in front of her, my hands settling on her waist. "I'm not walking away."

Her hand settles on my arm, tiny, warm, her touch right in ways no woman ever has been. "Good to know," she says. "Because I'm done hiding the monsters in the closet. If you can handle mine, I can handle yours."

She won't have to, I think. I won't let that happen. I won't put that shit on her. I drag her to me. "There are many things I want to say to you right now that are better said alone." The door opens behind me and Carrie and Reid's dog darts past us. My sister laughs and Reese's voice follows.

Abbie laughs, too, and when she looks at me, there is a swell of emotion between us that says more than words and it's not just about sex. We're connected. We're the real deal. I take her hand in mine and we greet Cat and Reese, with conversation veering toward Cat's *Cat Does Crime* syndicated column.

"Wait," Abbie says, as we all walk into the kitchen. "You're *Cat Does Crime*? Of course you are. I just—you're so involved in Reese's work that I didn't connect the dots. I love your column."

The two chat about Cat covering Reese's case in her particular editor voice and a few minutes later, the entire crew of Maxwells is sitting in the living room. Me and Abbie on the couch. Cat and Reese on an oversized chair to our left. My brother and Carrie on the chair across from us. Their adorable dog is at their feet, while the cat remains incognito. I actually miss Dexter right now. In a perfect world, I'd be home right now with my dog and my woman, and past all of this. But life and murder doesn't happen that easily.

"The good news," Reese says, loosening his navy striped tie, his jacket left behind in the kitchen. "I believe they've homed in on a suspect and if that were either of you, you'd be downtown right now. That being said, they aren't backing off on official interviews and they're being cryptic. They won't say where they sit on any theory about the murder. We're going into the interviews blind."

"When?" Abbie asks.

"The day after tomorrow because that's when I could make it work," Reese says. "And that gives us tomorrow to do some prep. We aren't back in court until noon tomorrow. I'd like to spend the morning with you both, prepping."

"They wouldn't interview us for no reason," Abbie says. "I mean, the inside word from Walker was that this is an assassination. Anyone could have ordered it."

"They'll look at your phone, electronic communications, and bank records. They'll ask us for them." He looks between us. "Either of you have an issue with that?"

"I don't," I say, my hand closing down on Abbie's leg. "Abbie?"

"I'm worried about that call I made to Jean Claude," she says. "And the email we exchanged afterward."

"We'll tell them about it," Reese says. "I'll prep you on everything tomorrow at my office."

"I'll be there to help," Cat offers, her hand on her pregnant belly.

"As will we," Reid offers of himself and Carrie. "But you need to be prepared for us to drill the hell out of you. That way when it happens with the police, you'll be ready."

Abbie inhales and presses her hands to her face before dropping them. "I can't believe he's dead and I'm having to go through this. It's like the hell that was this man will never end. He just reaches out of the grave and wraps his hand around my throat."

"You need to try to relax," Reese replies. "This may well be over when the interview is over. That's always the goal."

"What about the funeral?" she asks. "Should I go?"

Reese's reply is rapid fire. "Would you go if it was a heart attack?"

Her brow furrows. "No, I don't think—I don't know. Maybe. Maybe not. I'd probably fret over it."

"Then fret about it," Reese says, "and make the decision outside of the murder. Not going to a funeral doesn't make you guilty of murder."

"I don't know if I'd fucking go to our father's funeral," Reid grumbles.

"Don't say that," Cat chides.

"Look at the hell he's dragged us into, Cat," Reid counters. "And on top of that, he has someone trying to squeeze us for money, saying she has goods on him and his dirty laundry, of which we know there is much."

Thank you, Reid, I think, *for sharing details about our father I wasn't ready to disclose.* And right after he pretty much said I was an asshole that might not ever change while Abbie listened in.

"Oh my god," Cat says. "How did either of you not see him for what he is all those years?"

"A boy wants to idolize his father," Carrie chimes in. "I think they both just needed him to be more than he was."

"So did our mother," Cat replies, "but I know you know that."

"Of course," Carrie says. "You know I know."

"My question is: can he drag us all down with Abbie's ex?" Cat says. "I mean, could he have set you all up to look like you did this by way of a company transaction? How much access does he still have?"

My gaze rockets to Reid's. "He doesn't. Right?"

Reid sits up a little straighter. "Suddenly I want to have Blake do a wide search and make sure there's nothing with our names on it that we don't know about." He doesn't wait for my approval, which he has. He pulls out his phone and makes the call on speaker, explaining his worries.

"I'm not where I can get on this now," Blake says. "Give me a few hours, but I'll let you know tonight."

Reid disconnects the line and we all consider our worries. "I don't think he'd set us up," Reid says. "That would fuck his namesake."

"It could get you out of the picture," Cat says.

"Oh God," Carrie murmurs. "You just kicked him out of the firm. Even a charge could ensure he needs to come back to satisfy the board."

"Holy fuck," Reid and I say at the same moment.

Abbie stands up and I'm on my feet in a heartbeat, facing her. "Please tell me I didn't give him a free pass to hurt you? Please tell me I didn't ruin you?"

I cup her face. "Easy, Abbie, baby. We're okay. Our father can't win. He won't win."

"You're telling me you think he might really have done this? Is he capable of such a thing?"

I don't want to answer her. I don't want her to know that my father, the man I'm a spawn of, is capable of such evil, but now is not the time to protect her from the truth. "Yes.

Yes, I believe my father capable of such a thing. I believe he'd do anything to win and come out on top."

"Even murder Kenneth and frame his own sons?"

"Yes, baby, even that."

"No."

"Yes."

"I can't let this happen to you."

"We don't know anything right now. This is speculation done to protect ourselves. And you. I'm going to protect you."

She twists away from me and goes down on her knees in front of Cat and Reese. "Protect them. I'll get another attorney. Please protect them even if you have to throw me under the bus."

My heart squeezes. The only woman I've ever let close to me all but buried me. This one, this one, would bury herself for me. And I won't let her.

CHAPTER ELEVEN

gabe

Before I can even reach for Abbie, Cat is leaning toward her where she still kneels, drawing her hand into hers. "Honey," Cat declares, "my father doesn't get to destroy you or my brothers. He doesn't get to win because he's an ass and not only that, but I'm married to the best defense attorney on the planet, who is your attorney until this is over."

"We're not deserting you," Reese chimes in. "That's not how we operate."

"You can't represent me if I don't hire you," Abbie replies. "I'm not hiring you. That's official." She stands up and turns, running right into me.

I catch her arms, repeating Cat's declaration in my own words. "My father doesn't get to destroy any of us."

She grabs my shirt. "I told you to walk away."

"My father might have dragged me into this anyway. We're all better off with a united front. And we have your mother to think about, too."

"We?" she queries.

"We," I confirm, and as I expect with this group, everyone in the room chimes in and murmurs, "We."

"This is how we do things," I add. "We protect our own."

The forlorn look in those green eyes of hers says what she doesn't: *I'm not one of you.*

I lean in, my cheek pressed to hers, lips at her ear. "You're with me. You're with us."

"It's our way because it was our mother's way," Cat adds. "My mother was good and wonderful. This is what she would want. For us to stand together and with you. We're stronger together."

"Exactly why my father served you those papers," I say softly, for her ears only. "He was trying to divide us. Divided, he wins. Together, we win. All in together, Abbie. From this point forward, all in. Say it."

"Gabe," she breathes out.

"Say it."

"Yes," she says. "I'm all in."

I don't give her time to doubt that declaration. I turn her to face the room. "She's with us."

"Am I re-hired, Abbie?" Reese queries.

"Are you sure you want to be?" she asks.

"Completely," Reese replies without hesitation. "This is what I do. Help innocent people."

"Your mother's on her way," Reid announces. "The driver that picked her up just texted me. How's she handling this? Where's her head right now?"

Abbie settles back down on the couch next to me. "She's worried about me and she's worried about the animals at the shelter."

"Talk to me about the shelter," Reese says. "You have absolutely no idea why Jean Claude wants it?"

"None," Abbie says. "My ex gave it up easily in the divorce."

"Walker is trying to figure out why that property is in demand," I explain. "No luck so far. It could have been personal, a way for her ex to lash out at her."

"Which makes it look like I set him up with Jean Claude to end this," Abbie worries. "And really I did, but I didn't think that meant murder."

"I need a copy of the email you said followed the call," Reese says, and Abbie nods, pulling out her phone and punching a few buttons. She then shows me the email.

I read the short, to the point message and hand it to Reese. "She made no solicitation for murder at all."

"It's nothing more than the document that proved Kenneth was stealing from him," Abbie adds.

Reese accepts the phone, reads the message and then glances at Abbie. "Can I email this to myself?"

She nods. "Of course."

Reese sends the message to himself and right as he would hand the phone back to Abbie, Cat reaches for it. "Let me put our numbers in your phone," Cat offers. "Is that okay?"

Abbie nods. "Yes, please. Great."

"Ours, too, please," Carrie says. "Pass me the phone and I can put ours in."

"I've got it," Cat offers.

"You aren't saying anything about the email," Abbie worries, shoving wisps of red curls from her face to study Reese.

"Gabe is right," Reese replies. "You didn't solicit murder. You simply sent him the documents. If Jean Claude chose to react to the information you provided by killing Kenneth, no sane person does such a thing. No sane person expects such a thing. You have no reason to believe him capable of such a thing, which will be your defense."

"Right," she says, and while there is nothing wrong with her tone, I know where this is going.

My hand comes down on her leg. "You have to tell him."

"I do," she says. "I just—I can't seem," she looks at me, "to find the words."

I caress her cheek. "He needs you to just be straight with him."

"He wants innocence. Saying this out loud doesn't feel innocent."

"What is *this*?" Reese prods, interjecting himself with a hint of urgency in his tone. "What don't I know?"

I take control. I give him what he wants and needs, and what I know Abbie is going to choke on if I force her to share it herself. "She knew what Jean Claude was capable of. That's why she tried to get me to back out of this. She was worried that if I caused trouble for him, that I'd end up dead." I press my hand to her leg and refocus on Abbie. "You are one of the best people I know, outside of my sister. This doesn't make you guilty."

Her lips press together. "Doesn't it?"

"No, baby," I say softly. "It doesn't."

"Did you think Jean Claude would kill him, Abbie?"

"No."

"Did you believe that he was capable of murder?"

"Yes," she whispers. Her fingers curl on the edge of the cushion. "Kenneth would threaten me. *'Don't make me go to Jean Claude about you. He kills people who fuck with him.'*"

"Oh my God," Cat murmurs but Abbie doesn't look at her. She focuses on Reese.

"I really didn't think he'd kill him," she says, "but now I sound really guilty."

Reese studies her for an eternal second and no one pushes him. Reese wasn't joking about his moral compass. He doesn't represent people he doesn't trust or believe to be innocent. He stands up and walks a few steps before he turns to face us, his hands settling on his hips. "Did you know any names? Was there someone Jean Claude was supposed to have killed?"

"No," Abbie says. "It wasn't like that. It was more my ex talking big. He did a lot of talking big. Like I said, he used Jean Claude to scare me."

"Fuck," I murmur. "If he wasn't dead, I'd fucking kill him."

"Amen to that," Reid adds.

"I might help," Carrie chimes in. "What an asshole." She slides her hand to Reid's. "Thank God you got away from that man before he pulled you down."

"We'll figure it out," Reese says, tuning us out, and focusing solely on Abbie, "if this gets pointed your direction. It may not. We'll prepare tomorrow. We'll be ready for anything."

Abbie breathes out. "Then you're still with me?"

"I'm with you," Reese says, with no hesitation, but the lines of his face are drawn tight, his tone harrowed. I know this man. He's worried for us. I wasn't. I knew there was nothing that could come back on us, but Abbie's past with her ex is riddled with motives. And mine is riddled with my father, who won't just go the fuck away. It might be time to start to get worried.

LISA RENEE JONES

CHAPTER TWELVE

gabe

I'm still contemplating the levels of hell my father might travel to drag us there with him when Cat pops to her feet, drawing everyone's attention as she exclaims, "I see everyone in this room worrying right now and this is ridiculous. We need to just go talk to dad and end this."

Abbie casts me a hopeful look. "Is that an option? I didn't think that was an option."

"No," I say, at the same time as Reid and now the entire room is standing.

"You're not going to see your father," Reese orders, on his feet and catching Cat's hand, grounding her right here in their home. "You and our baby don't need that stress."

"Worrying like this is stressful," she replies. "Let's just end it." She twists around to face us all. "End it. Let's confront him."

"If anyone was going to confront him, it would be me," Reid replies. "I'm not personally involved. He sees me as the cold-hearted bastard I can be."

"Neither am I," Cat argues. "I'm not involved."

"When you get involved, we look rattled," I interject. "He doesn't need to see us as rattled."

"Exactly," Reid states. "Calculated is more like it, and calculated means we wait to see what Blake has to say about any tricks he might have played to frame us."

"We don't need to give him ideas," I agree. "For all we know, the police are looking at him right now." I eye Cat's belly pointedly. "Protect what's important. Reid and I will deal with our bastard of a father who should be protecting you, too, but won't."

The doorbell rings. "That's Abbie's mother," Reid says. "Walker has the security clearance to bring her up."

I turn to Abbie, my hands settling on her shoulders. "Be strong and she'll be strong."

"I will be," she promises. "I don't want her to panic."

"You also need to allow Reese to talk to her without you protecting her. Just like I had to do with you."

"Yes," Reese states. "I need to be clear, Abbie. I'm representing you with the family right now. I'm not promising to represent your mother. I met her at the shelter. I liked her, but I need to talk to her before I make a commitment."

"Thank you for considering her as a client," Abbie says. "She's a good person, but she's also—"

"Abigail!"

At the sound of her mother's voice, Abbie rotates and takes off around the couch. I watch as the two of them collide into a hug just outside of the line of the living area. "That bastard can't even die without making your life hell," her mother growls.

Abbie gasps and speaks to her mother in a low voice. I eye Reese, who gives me a small smile that tells me he gets it. She's protecting her daughter. He motions me to join him. "Let's go to the kitchen," he says, kissing Cat as Reid catches her arm and urges her to stay behind. I know my brother. He's going to talk our sister off the ledge our father will shove her off of.

A few minutes later, me, Reese, Abbie, and her mother are in the kitchen standing around the island.

"You're the best of the best, I hear," Abbie's mother says to Reese. She looks tired, her red hair a tangled mess, dark circles shadowing her eyes. "I already knew you were generous and that you love animals, considering your help at the shelter. You're a good man. Thank you for helping."

"I try to be," Reese says. "And what was Abbie's ex? What kind of man was he?"

"He was no man. He was a monster."

"You hated him," Reese states.

Abbie's mom doesn't hesitate. "With all my heart and soul, but I suspect that man has plenty of people who feel that way. I don't think lying about it serves a purpose besides making me look like a liar."

"She's always brutally honest," Abbie offers. "I was going to warn you about that."

Reese's attention falls on Abbie. "Let me have a word with your mother alone."

Abbie's spine stiffens. "Yes—but—"

I stroke her hair. "Abbie, baby—"

"I'm good, honey," her mother assures her. "Let me talk to Reese."

"You're sure?" Abbie asks. "Because I know this is overwhelming and—"

"Abigail, give me some credit. I save dying animals a few days a week. I can handle a little pressure. I'm more worried about you than me. Let me talk to Reese."

"I'll take good care of her," Reese promises.

Abbie inhales and nods at the room in general. "Yes. Okay."

I don't give her time to change her mind. I lace my fingers with Abbie's and lead her out of the kitchen to the hallway just off the foyer. It's the perfect time for us to have a serious talk. For that reason, my intended destination is Reese's home office on the other side of the apartment, but Abbie spies the bathroom, she darts away from me and inside. Running. She's always running and it's time to end that and a few other things while we're at it. I'm on her heels and before she can shut the bathroom door, I'm inside the tiny visitor-sized space with her, shutting the door and locking it.

"Oh my God, Gabe," Abbie whispers urgently. "What are you doing?"

I turn to face her, pulling her to me and then rotating her, placing her against the door. "Do not do what you did out there ever again."

"Even if I knew what you meant, you don't get to order me around in your sister's bathroom, Gabe."

"On this I do, baby. Don't throw yourself under the train for me. I can hold back the train, but once you're underneath, I can't pull you back up. Do you understand?"

Her eyes spark with anger, a stubborn set to her jaw. "No. No, I don't understand. And to be clear, the reverse of what you just said is true. Once you're under the train—"

"That won't happen." I cup her backside and pull her to me. "I won't go under unless you force me under, and the way you do that is by forcing me to save you by throwing myself there."

"I'm trying to save you, not throw you under, Gabe. I heard the fear in your sister's voice. I saw the fear in her eyes. She believes your father will take you down. She believes he can."

"My sister doesn't like to see how capable her brothers are of fighting a man like our father. You heard what Reid said to me in the hallway. There's a part of me you don't know and I don't want you to know, Abbie. That part of me will win, which means you win and you're free."

"What part of you, Gabe? What does that even mean?"

"Why? Ready to run? I thought you weren't going to run, Abbie."

"What part of me asking a question says that I'm running? Did I say I was running?"

"You ran into this bathroom."

"I have to pee, which I can't do with your hand on my ass and your big body on top of mine. Or with you watching. And you know what?" She pokes my chest. "After I overheard Reid talking to you, I said I wasn't going to run because you didn't deny what your brother said. You didn't deny a past that he knows and worries about. You didn't tell me I didn't understand what I heard when we both know I did. That felt honest. I need honesty in my life. Be honest with me and if you aren't, I won't run away, but I will walk away. Be you, because I can't deal with another man who seems like one thing but turns out to be another."

Be me.

Be honest.

She wouldn't like the truth I have to hide, not my truth, but I don't say this. She won't accept it. Instead, I choose to be honest about what I can be, what I'm willing to disclose. "You want honest? When I said any man could fall in love with you, I meant me. *I* could fall in love with you, Abbie, if you give me the chance, but I won't get that chance if you take a fall for me that I don't need you to take."

And then I dare to ask for what I don't deserve to hear the answer to, considering how quickly I've just avoided the real truth of who and what I am. "I need you to trust me. *Really* trust me. I need us to be a team. You and me, baby. We fight this together. Remember? That's our word: together."

LISA RENEE JONES

CHAPTER THIRTEEN

gabe

Seconds tick by and Abbie just stares up at me. She doesn't speak. She doesn't snap back as she has been the past ten minutes. The small guest bathroom of my sister's apartment shrinks, my near declaration of love hanging in the air between us, obviously not well received. I give a choked laugh. "You wanted honest? You got love, baby. That's as damn honest as it gets."

"Don't. Don't fall in love, Gabe. Love is ugly. It cuts and it makes you bleed and—"

I cup her head and stare down at her. "I will never cut you and I will never make you bleed."

"No one thinks that's how love will treat them," she says. "But then they're crying bloody damn tears."

She's afraid.

I should be afraid. Hell, I have as many reasons as she has to punch a hole through love, but it doesn't seem to matter. I can't seem to shut down with this woman. "I'm not doing this alone, Abbie. If I'm falling, you're falling with me."

Her fingers curl on my chest. "I won't fall, Gabe."

"I'll catch you. Give me the chance, and you'll see that I'll catch you. Hell, I'm trying to show you that now."

"You—are wonderful. You've been nothing *but* wonderful."

I narrow my eyes on her. "But?"

"No buts. That's a fact."

"He was wonderful at first, too," I say, understanding washing over me.

"Not in the Gabe kind of way. He was debonair and charming, but he wasn't you. I don't mean to judge you by him, because that's not fair."

"What's the Gabe kind of way, Abbie?"

"You're funny and sweet and yet so damn protective. He was never those things. He was flowers and jewelry, and nothing more. Superficial things that meant nothing."

"You want flowers and jewelry."

"Don't turn me being honest into that, Gabe. I don't care about flowers and jewelry. I said those things don't matter."

"I can give you those things and more. I haven't had time."

"You already have."

"And yet you want me to fall alone?"

"No. God, no. I *want* you to be the man of my dreams and that is some scary shit, Gabe. I don't really know you."

"You know more than you think."

"I know you're determined to keep a part of you locked away and it's not even fair for me to ask you to share those parts of yourself right now. We're new and—I have no right."

But one day, she will. She doesn't have to say that. It's true. She will but that doesn't mean I'm going to go all those deep dark places with her. "Some things don't matter. Especially when someone comes along and shows them that they don't matter."

"I don't know what that means."

"It means I'm different with you, baby, and that's a good thing." I pull her hand between us and kiss it. "Go to the bathroom. We'll talk later when we're finally alone. I'll be outside waiting for you." I reach for the door and she catches my arm.

"What about my mother? Where will she go tonight?"

"She can go home or she can come to my place. What will she want? What do *you* want?"

"She won't go to your place. She's very independent, but I'm worried about the police cornering her."

"Reese will handle that and I'm sure he'll schedule an interview for her as he did for us. But if Reese feels she should stay with us, we'll force the issue."

Her eyes soften. "Thank you, Gabe."

"You don't have to thank me. We're—"

Her lips are pressed to my lips, and I don't need further invitation. I cup her head and kiss the hell out of her, but the thing is, she kisses the hell out of me, too. I am instantly hot and hard, and it's all I can do not to turn her to the sink, pull up her skirt and find my way inside her, but now is not the time nor the place.

"You, woman, are definitely trying to make me fall," I say, releasing her and exiting the bathroom to find Reid sitting on the stairs a few feet away, waiting on me.

"How's Cat?" I ask, claiming the step next to him.

"She's Cat. Ready to save the world and us. On another note. I heard from Blake. He doesn't see anything electronically that looks like trouble for either of us."

"That's good news." Only he's scowling. "What?"

"There's an account in Abbie's name that, while inactive now, had a large sum of money in it at one point."

"The point? Aside from the fact that she was married to a billionaire."

"It has some funny transactions that might be money laundering," he says.

"Holy fuck." I scrub my jaw and lower my voice. "Can Blake make this go away?"

"He already did, but there's more. There's a connection between that account and—"

"Our father," I say, instantly realizing where this is going.

Reid gives a sharp nod. "Yes. Our father. "

"This explains so damn much. He served her a phony lawsuit under our company. I called his bluff, but clearly, he's motivated to scare her away from me. Because this all runs too close to home, his home, for his comfort." I grimace. "I wonder if Abbie will love me or hate me when she finds out that I killed my own damn father."

"I could make it easy on you," Reid offers. "I could do it for you."

Only he won't. He has a wife to think about. I, on the other hand, have Abbie to save. I'm not sure that's going to work out so well for my father.

CHAPTER FOURTEEN

gabe

Reid and I are still sitting on the stairwell of Cat and Reese's apartment when Carrie rounds the corner. "What's going on with the Maxwell brothers?"

"Just talking about our dark side," Reid replies, the dark side being our father.

Abbie exits the bathroom at the same time and manages to hear what was said. "Dark side? Oh do tell."

I stand up and before I can reply, Carrie answers for us. "That would be their father, the monster, who they fantasize about slaying. As do I. He tried to destroy me and my father."

Abbie's stare rockets to mine, and it's her inspection now that feels dark. Abbie now knows, without a shadow of a doubt, that the same kind of evil that's in her ex's blood is in mine. "He's that bad?"

"Worse," I say, seeing no point in holding back now. My father's a prick worthy of a public announcement.

"Can we talk a minute alone?" Abbie asks, and since we just talked alone in the bathroom, I assume my father, the prick, has her attention.

"We're all done!"

It's Abbie's mother, who enters the hallway, and suddenly it's a family fucking meeting in the hallway. That alone talk between me and Abbie isn't happening, which means whatever she is thinking right now is going to simmer and brew. Especially since her mother is now standing in front of her. "Let's step outside a minute," her mother suggests, her body now between me and Abbie, blocking any chance I have to see Abbie's expression. And then, fuck, they're walking away. I do the same. To the damn kitchen.

I find Reese and Cat standing on the opposite side of the island and I join them, taking advantage of my first chance to talk to Reese alone since this happened. "What are you thinking?"

I'm talking to Reese, but Cat answers. "That we have the worst father on planet earth. That I still want to go see him and just deal with this."

"And you know why that isn't an option." I change the subject with a forceful push in another direction. I look at Reese. "What are *you* thinking?"

"That your father is the biggest bastard I've ever known and I've known some bastardly people. As for Abbie and her mother, they're good people. I'll get them through the interviews and we'll hope they need nothing more." He leans closer, lowering his voice. "Is there anything I need to know?"

"I talked with her ex this weekend. We fought."

"About what?"

"He was harassing Abbie. I didn't let that continue."

"What did you do to stop that from happening?"

"Gabe told him that he'd fuck him without Vaseline," Abbie says from the door. "I may or may not have gotten those words one hundred percent right. I think there was something about bending him over, as well."

"Bending over was definitely suggested," I confirm, "but no one actually bent over."

"He could have recorded your call," Cat says. "You can't assume this isn't a problem."

Abbie steps to my side. "He took the phone because Kenneth was harassing me."

"Harassing you how?" Reese asks.

"He told me to get rid of Gabe or he'd make my life hell. He was all but stalking me. He even broke into my apartment and left my wedding ring on the bed."

"Wait," Cat says. "When?"

Abbie replays the entire incident, and eyes Reese. "You don't look happy."

"This all complicates our interview responses," he says. "It's good you told me but I need to think about how I'm going to guide you to answer, or not answer, certain questions. We'll prep tomorrow. Everyone needs to get some rest tonight."

"And food," Cat says. "No one ordered me and my baby pizza."

I round the island and hug her. "Pizza and ice cream next time." I lean in and whisper, "Don't let dad work you up. He's not worth it."

"But you and Reid are," she says, her voice cracking. "Be careful."

I nod, wishing I could have kept her out of this, and knowing it's time to give her space. I catch Abbie's eye and motion toward the door. "Where's your mother? Does she need a ride?"

"Would you believe that billionaire rancher from the Hamptons is here with her? She left. They have dinner plans."

She left Abbie during this mess? That hits me ten shades of wrong I don't voice. "We do, too," I say, thinking I might try to convince her to eat pizza naked in bed. It'll give new meaning to pizza for me.

We say our goodbyes, grab our coats, and once we're in the hallway, I turn Abbie to face me. "You had something you wanted to say to me?"

"Yes. I did. I do."

"Well?"

"Not here. Not now. Alone."

And yet she wanted to have the talk here a few minutes ago. "Tell me now."

"No," she says, and she starts walking toward the elevator.

And I follow, because a) she has a mighty fine ass, and b) I want to. I'm in trouble with this woman and I fucking love it.

CHAPTER FIFTEEN

gabe

The minute Abbie and I enter the elevator, I punch in the lobby level and then drag her to me, my hand at the back of her head. "How's this for talking?" I ask a moment before my mouth closes down on hers, my tongue licking past her lips, drinking her in, tasting her.

She pushes against my chest, moans, sinks into the kiss, but ultimately, when we reach the lobby and our lips part, she doesn't mince words. "That's not talking. That's deflection. We need to talk. *Really* talk."

"We did talk, baby. We just spoke volumes by kissing instead of yelling."

"Talk, Gabe. Real conversation."

"I'm all about real with you, Abbie," I say, which is true. What I say to her is real. I just don't say all there is to say. "And we'll talk. At my place."

"Yes," she says, offering that confirmation. "At your place."

The doors open and I lace the fingers of one of her hands with mine, leading her into the hallway and outside to our hired car. She slides into the backseat, and I follow, sealing us inside without missing a beat. My hand comes down on her leg and I drag her close. She doesn't push me away. Her hand comes down on my hand, her eyes lifting to meet mine. "Gabe," she whispers.

"Just to be clear. Are we fighting?"

Her hand settles on my cheek. "Maybe. We can decide when we get to your apartment."

I laugh. She laughs. There is a warm intimacy between us, but it doesn't erase the fact that she wants to have that "alone" talk. That she wants answers to questions I can only assume were created by being around my family. I kiss her hand, settling it on my leg, my hand covering hers now. She's still going to hit me on the conversations she overheard tonight between me and Reid. She's still going to want answers I'm not eager to offer but after the past few hours, I'm of the mind that I can't keep as much of me to myself as I'd planned with Abbie. Not if I want her in my life. The question is, how much is too much of me, this soon, for Abbie?

A few minutes later, we pull up to my apartment, and it's not as simple as taking her upstairs and just fucking her until she forgets why she wants because one: she's Abbie. I want more than that with her. And two: Dexter needs to pee and eat. The damn dog who greets us with ridiculous happiness and kisses. "You're blowing your serial killer reputation, bud," I say, as I squat down to give him some love. "Seriously, man. You need to keep the story going." I stand up to Abbie's assuming stare.

"You and Dexter," she says. "Two men with more to you than meets the eye. Is that what drew you to him?"

"I do believe you've hit the nail on the head," I say, because no matter how silly the moment, there's an element of honesty there but I still finish off with a wink and a compliment. "You mad genius you."

Dexter barks his agreement or maybe he just really needs to pee like a Russian Race Horse. "Yes, killer," I say. "We're going out." I wink at Abbie and motion to the door. "Walk with us?"

"Of course," she says, warmth in her eyes that tells a story. She likes that I was honest. She needs honesty in her life. I want to be honest with her. I *have* to be honest with her. In every possible way I can be without losing her in the process.

After a quick change to casual clothes, with Dexter's supervision of course, we head out. I open the front door and Dexter darts for the hall. "Stop," I order.

Dexter stops and looks back at me, impatience in his gaze. "Ladies first," I tell him "Sit and wait." Dexter proves he's had some training because he does as he's told; he sits and waits.

Abbie laughs. "Impressively submissive for a serial killer." She heads into the hallway and turns to eye us both. "Come to me, you handsome man, you."

"Me or Dexter?" I ask.

"Both of you. Come to me, you handsome men, you."

Dexter looks up at me and whines, showing great restraint considering he wants to hurry to Abbie's side, and with good reason. She's fucking beautiful, all that red hair wild and free right now. Her smile touching her eyes, lighting her heart-shaped face. "Go, boy," I say.

Dexter barks his approval again and rushes toward Abbie. She kneels and greets him and he rewards her with sloppy doggy kisses. The only woman I'd kiss after a dog. I'm pretty sure that means I'm right again. I'm falling in love. I exit to join them and help Abbie to her feet, pulling her to me, her body aligned with mine, nice and tight. "Did I ever tell you that I don't like redheads?"

She laughs. "What are you talking about?"

"Just what I said. I'm not a guy who goes for redheads. Except you, Abbie," I say, and my joking moment has gotten all hot and serious, my voice lowering as I add, "You're really fucking beautiful. Too beautiful for my own good."

"But you don't like redheads?"

"Nope. Never. I'm a changed man now, though, and that's all about you."

"Gabe," she whispers, her eyes going all soft and willing while I go all hot and hard.

Dexter whines and Abbie tugs my arm. "He needs to go out."

"Yes, the little beast needs to go out."

I kiss her and we hurry toward the elevator. A few minutes later we're at the park a block away and Dexter is sniffing everything in sight. Abbie and I stand together and watch him. "I should probably hire a permanent dog walker to come in twice a day."

"From rescue to spoiled king," Abbie says. "I love it." She turns to face me. "Gabe, I really do love so much about you." Her fingers curl on my chest. "But I need to know the man I'm falling for really is the man I think he is."

"I am. I'm me. I'm just me."

"I heard enough today at your sister's to know that you're not all jokes and fun. I heard that with your interaction with Kenneth." I open my mouth to reply but she quiets me with a hand. "Carrie is Reid's compass. I sensed that in her and him. If you want us to make it, you have to trust me the way he trusts her. Eventually. Not now. I know that, but eventually."

Eventually is too soon, considering my past but I can't say that to her. "One day at a time. Okay?"

"As long as those days are honest days, Gabe, I can handle almost anything. Except one thing: lies. I can't handle lies. If you, this person you are with me, is a lie, tell me. End it now."

My hand slides under her hair, settling on her neck. "I told you, Abbie, I'm more real with you than I have ever been with anyone."

"*More* real. Not real."

"Everything I show you, everything we share, is real."

"The parts you show me, excluding the part of you that you think I'll hate, of course."

My expression tightens. "The part of me that I *know* you'll hate."

"The part you believe is your father. That was the talk I wanted to have and this is what I wanted to say to you. You are not your father. I will never see him in you."

Until she does, I think. "Never make a promise you can't keep, baby."

LISA RENEE JONES

CHAPTER SIXTEEN

abbie

Gabe and I move on from our "talk," enjoying our walk with Dexter and all of his silly antics. It's laughter and fun. It's an escape and I find myself not wanting this part of the day to end. Dexter seems to agree, as he takes off running and Gabe curses. "Oh hell. Why'd I let him off leash?" Gabe takes off running now, too. I laugh because Dexter turns around and charges at Gabe. In what feels like a few blinks, Gabe is on his back and Dexter is on top of him. I hurry toward them and go down on my knees, only to be tackled by Dexter, too.

"Dexter!" Gabe chides, pulling him off of me, but not before I get a tongue bath. "My tongue," Gabe says, "her mouth. Not your tongue." He grabs my hand and sits me up. "You okay, baby?"

Baby.

It's not the first time he's called me this, but now, in this moment, that small endearment does big, fluttery things to my belly. "Yes, I say. "I'm great. Actually, really great." I brush grass from his hair. "Dexter's pretty wonderful." *And so are you, Gabe,* I think, *so are you.*

"Yeah," he agrees, his eyes warming. "He is and so are you."

"Tell me that when you know me better," I tease, pleased that he's said what I was thinking about him. "I have bad habits."

"Tell me about these bad habits," he says, as Dexter plops down on the ground next to us, and a cold breeze blasts over us.

I shiver and Gabe stands, taking me with him. "Tell me at home in the warm apartment."

At home. His home. But I like that he calls it home. I like that he's invited me into a place that is his castle. His private space. We link our arms together and start walking.

"About those bad habits," he says. "You tell me yours. I'll tell you mine."

"I'm messy," I say. "I'm bad about leaving my shoes by the bed and not in the closet. Stuff like that. And my hair is wild in the mornings." I give him a coy look. "But you know that."

"Your hair is sexy as fuck in the morning."

"But you don't like redheads, right?" I tease.

"You're it, Abbie. You're exactly what I like. Even if you don't know it yet." He leans into me and presses his lips to mine. "I'll show you upstairs."

I smile. God how easily he makes me smile. "Promise?" I whisper.

"I never make a promise I don't keep."

It's a light moment, invaded by a flicker of a memory of him talking to my ex, of his promises to hurt Kenneth; of my certainty then in that moment, that Gabe could hold his own with a brutal man like Kenneth. I wait for this to bother me, but it doesn't. I admire his strength. I like that he's protective. I like *him*. *I am* falling for him. I might truly fall in love with him.

I shove aside thoughts of Kenneth but as soon we arrive back at Gabe's building a thirty-something man with a stubble roughened jawline, steps in front of us. "Abigail Tanner?"

I stiffen and Gabe's fingers flex on my hip. "Who are you?" he asks and Dexter must sense our discomfort because he snarls and starts to growl.

The man, whose trench coat could be hiding a weapon, holds out his hands. "Easy there, puppy."

I want to say good boy, I really do. My ex was murdered. Until now, it never crossed my mind that someone might want me dead as well. I was his wife. I was linked to him for five years.

"He doesn't like it when you call him a puppy," Gabe snaps. "In fact, it really pisses him off. Almost as much as strangers showing up outside my apartment. Who are you and what do you want?" Dexter snarls louder, Gabe tightening his hold on him, or I'm pretty sure he'd live up to his killer name.

"I'm a reporter for the NY News," he says. "I have credentials." He motions to his coat. "I can show you."

"Credentials or a gun?" I demand. "How do we know which you're reaching for?"

"A reasonable fear," the man concludes, "especially considering your ex-husband was killed execution-style. I'm sure you're afraid you're next."

And there it is. He's confirming my new fear that I don't want confirmed. "You're digging for information we don't have to give," Gabe snaps. "We have nothing to say to you." Gabe turns me and Dexter toward the building.

The man calls out, "You're the new man, Mr. Maxwell. Were you jealous? Did you kill him?"

My heart squeezes and I feel like it's being ripped out of my chest. I don't want this for Gabe. It's so unfair. He doesn't deserve to be treated like this. I rotate and scowl. I open my mouth to speak, but Gabe turns me to face him. "Don't say a word. That's what he wants. To goad you into saying something he can print. Walk away. Together. Let's walk away together."

The doorman appears by our side, as the reporter calls out, "You spoke to him the night before he died! I know you spoke to him, Gabe Maxwell. Did you fight?"

Gabe's jaw sets hard and the big, burly doorman rushes to our sides. "You want me to deal with him?"

"Yes, Steven," Gabe replies. "The sooner the fucking better." He palms him a large bill.

"Consider him handled and please, take shelter inside and enjoy your evening."

Dexter thanks him by licking his hand. Steven offers the killer dog a tiny smile and pets him but Gabe is already leading us toward the building.

"Don't talk in the elevator," he warns, as we cross the lobby and he punches the call button. "We can't risk being recorded and we now know we have reporters charting our every move."

I nod, hating our perfect walk has become this. The elevator takes several ridiculously long minutes to arrive which I use to worry about Gabe and the attacks just thrown his direction. Once we're inside the car, Gabe punches in our floor, leans on the wall and to my relief, pulls me to him, holding me close. I rotate and wrap my arms around him. I hold him close, too.

CHAPTER SEVENTEEN

abbie

The minute we're off the elevator, Dexter is bounding down the hallway, apparently feeding off my need to be in a private spot where Gabe and I can speak. Gabe catches my hand and links our fingers, and miraculously, that easily, I can breathe again. Gabe does that for me. He calms me down. He makes me feel like I'm standing with him, while my ex was always above me.

He pulls out his keys and unlocks the door. The minute it's open, he unhooks Dexter, who bounds forward again with panting glee. He's home and that dog knows it. I feel oddly good about being at home here, too, but that's all the more reason for me to worry about Gabe. To worry about his family. It's my turn to bound into the hallway and I do so, but leave out the panting. I rotate to face Gabe, and he's shut the door, already right in front of me, his hands settling possessively at my waist.

"You need to stop worrying," he says. "I've got this. I've got you. I've got us." He turns me around and pulls off my coat.

"He's going to smear you in the press," I say, turning as he hangs up my coat on the coatrack, and shrugs out of his own. "He's going to make you look like a killer."

"He's not going to slander me," he replies. "That would land him in court. He's trying to intimidate us into talking. I don't intimidate."

"I'm worried about you, Gabe, even if you aren't."

"That's the point. He wants you to worry. He wants you to talk. He wants a story." He takes my hand. "Come with me."

He's clearly not listening. He's leading me through the living room, towards his obvious solution to our problems: the bar. Dexter is now sitting by the couch with a bone in his mouth, watching us pass by. I wave to him and he turns away as if he thinks I'm about to take his bone.

"Drink time," Gabe says lifting me and sitting me on a barstool.

"We've done this before. I don't drink well."

He steps behind the bar and pours me a whiskey. "Try it," he says, setting the glass in front of me. "Honey-sweet perfection, baby, like you on my tongue. We'll get that asshole off your mind, one way or another."

My cheeks heat. "Did you really just say that to me?"

He leans on the bar in front of me. "Would you rather me say it to someone else?"

There's a push between us with that question that is so much more than it appears on the surface. It's about commitment, about reassurance. "No," I say. "I do not want you to say anything even remotely like that to another woman."

"Did it bother you when I said it to you? Did it offend you?"

"No," I say easily. "No, it just took me off guard."

"Your ex didn't talk dirty to you?"

"Was that talking dirty?"

"That was a warm-up." He winks. "It gets better." He points at the glass. "Drink up, baby. You're wound as tight as a rubber band ball."

I accept the drink and decide he's right. I need to relax. I down the liquid, warmth spreading down my throat and settling low in my belly. "I felt that," I say, touching my throat.

"What do you feel?"

"Warm," I say. "Really warm."

He fills my glass again. "Drink a little more. Don't down it." He lifts a finger. "Not yet." He rounds the bar and walks into the kitchen, grabs something from the fridge and returns. He sets a can down next to me.

I inspect it. "Diet Sprite?"

"A man has to watch his waistline." He winks. "It's nice and smooth with the whiskey, or so my sister tells me. Before she got pregnant, of course." He mixes the drink for me.

I take a sip and the whiskey goes down smoother. "I approve. I like it."

He pours a glass for himself and then claims the stool next to mine, both of us facing each other, both of us sipping our drinks. His hand settles on my leg and I set my glass down. The whiskey wasn't what made me warm. It's him, all him.

"You," I whisper.

"You," he whispers. "Stay with me until this is over. And if that's three days from now, stay longer. I don't want you to leave any time soon. Hell, I might not want you to leave at all."

My heart swells with so many emotions, too many emotions. "We're moving fast, Gabe. So very fast."

"I know what I want," he says. "And that's you."

"You say that now, but wait until your firm is all over the news, and not in a good way, because of me."

"Not because of you. You didn't do this. My father was already involved in this."

"But you weren't."

"He was looking for a way to bite us back. He would have found a way no matter what. We expected a war. We hoped we wouldn't get one." He rests his forehead on mine, his hand settling at the back of my head. "I will handle my father." There is a rough quality to his voice that undoes me.

I pull back to look at him, his hand returning to my leg with his other. "He's your father. Would he really want to ruin you?"

"He's my father. Translation: yes."

"What Reid said to you in the hallway—about your dark side—" I hesitate with how to continue and he reacts.

His hands fall away from my legs and settle on his own. "What about it?"

I press my hands to his. "Don't tell me you want me here in your life, and then pull away from me. All in or all out, Gabe. I don't care about your father. I don't care about how dark you can get unless it includes killing people and hurting people just to hurt them. You're an attorney. You have a job to do, and I'm not naive. I know you have to be hard. I know you have—"

"You don't know, Abbie." He untangles his hands from mine and reaches for his drink. "And never going to know those parts of me. That won't change. If you can't live with that—"

"I can't. I can't live with that. All or nothing, and at the park, you said—"

"You can have all that I am *now*. Other parts are past and buried, where they need to stay."

Like the reason he had a vasectomy, I think, and I want to say it, but my gut says, that's pushing him too far, too fast. "Gabe—"

He downs his drink and stands up, walking to the window, where he's told me he stands above the city, to escape the rest of the world. To that spot he allowed me to visit with him. He let me into his space, his kingdom, his head, just not his past. He needs that to be enough. I scoot off the stool and he presses his hands to the glass. I close the space between us and slide between him and the window.

He responds instantly, tangling his fingers into my hair. "I won't ever show you that part of me. It exists. You know. Leave it the fuck alone."

Now I'm angry. He's holding me and pushing me away at the same time. "Because I'm weak? Because I'm this pathetic girl you need to save to feel like you aren't whatever monster you've decided to call yourself? Because I'm scared? Or maybe it's you who's scared? You're scared to show me the real you."

"Maybe there's a reason to be scared."

"Maybe you want me to be scared."

"You do like to run, Abbie."

My chin lifts defiantly. "I'm not running now, now am I?"

He stares down at me, intense seconds crackling between us before his mouth crashes down on mine; his big body pressing me against the steel railing, a wild desperate hunger in him that isn't gentle or funny as he can be, but rough, demanding, and edgy. This is the man who can be bad and I have this sense that he's about to test me. That he's about to show me the real Gabe Maxwell.

And I like it.

LISA RENEE JONES

CHAPTER EIGHTEEN

abbie

"What do you want, Abbie?" Gabe demands, tearing his mouth from mine. "Say it. I need you to be clear. What do you want? But be careful what you ask for. You'll get it."

"More," I say, twisting my hands in his T-shirt. "More of you, Gabe. All of you."

He slides his hands under my leggings, palming my backside I left bare in the rush to take out Dexter. "More doesn't get you a nice, funny guy, Abbie."

"Thank fuck for that. Show me. Stop hiding. Stop trying to be only what you think I want, Gabe. Stop trying to be less than you are because that makes us less than we can be."

"And if you can't handle who I am?"

I'm on fire now, poking the bear and I can't hold back. "And you're afraid to find out. Is fear all I make you feel?"

His mouth suddenly crashes down on mine once more, his tongue pressing past my teeth, his kiss demanding, angry. He's pissed. At me. At himself, I think, and that's what I want to know. That's the part of him I want to understand, I want to demand he show me.

"Get undressed," he orders, setting me back from him, crossing his arms in front of that broad perfect chest of his.

My chin lifts in defiance, in refusal to allow him to intimidate me. Maybe he wants me to think he's a monster like Kenneth. Maybe that should even piss me off but it doesn't. It challenges me.

I pull my shirt over my head and toss it aside. "See?" I say. "Sometimes I even follow orders." I unhook my bra, shrugging it away, exposing my naked breasts, the cold air puckering my nipples. "I must be very, very afraid of you." I toe off my shoes and peel away my leggings, no panties to fret with. I'm not wearing any. Naked now but for socks, I'm not messing with, I close the small space between us and stand in front of him. "Or maybe I was right. You're the one who's afraid."

He catches my hip and drags me to him. "You're playing with fire."

"Stop warning me away and pulling me back. Choose, Gabe. All in, remember? Or is that code for only if it's me?"

His jaw clenches, his gaze lowering, raking over my naked breasts, and I can't explain it, but I'm more naked right now, in this moment, with this man, than I've ever been before.

"All in, Abbie. That's what you want? That's what you'll get." He backs me up and presses my hands on the bar behind me and at my sides. He shackles my hips, and pulls me forward, forcing me to use them to hold myself up. "Keep your hands there," he orders. "If you move them, I'll punish you."

Heat rushes through me but there is no fear. I don't fear this man the way I feared Kenneth. I will never fear Gabe. I damn sure don't fear the thick bulge of his erection pressing against my belly. "Punish me?" I challenge. "How would you punish me, Gabe?"

"You still haven't been properly spanked, now have Abbie?"

"You spanked me, remember?"

"That was a love pat, *remember?* A spanking" he adds, most likely for effect, as he's watching me with hooded eyes. "My hands on your pretty little ass. My cock buried inside you while I make it burn."

His hand on my ass.

Spanking me.

His eyes lower to my mouth, linger with a promise of a kiss I crave but that doesn't come, his gaze lifting with his own challenge. "Are you scared now?"

"If that's the goal, it's safe to say that you failed. I'm pretty sure what's going on with me right now, can not be described as fear. Are *you scared*?"

I expect him to laugh or balk but he doesn't. He leans in close, his lips at my ear, "From the day I met you, baby. From the day I met you." He pulls back to look at me, blue eyes lit up and like fires in a forest, they burn a path through me. "And you're right. I am pushing you. Right here. Right now. Don't move."

He steps back from me, and obedience is easy this time. He undresses. I get to watch and watching Gabe get naked is a sight to see. He's long. He's lean. He's all muscle and that tattoo. That lion tattoo on his arm means more to me every time I see it. It's strength and family. It's him, the real him, the man willing to fight to win. And his cock, well, he's blessed in that department and so am I. His shaft juts forward, thick and heavily veined with arousal.

My teeth sink into my bottom lip, all this talking and watching about to undo me. I need him. I need him next to me. I need him touching me. I need him inside me. I just need him to touch me and thankfully he does. He pulls me forward, cups my ass, scrapes his teeth over the spot where mine had just been, nipping roughly.

I yelp and he cups my head. "Now for that spanking. You didn't think I'd forget, did you?"

"You really do want to scare me, don't you?"

He grips my hair, erotic and rough, and tugs my gaze to his. "No. I want to give you a reason to forget the fucked up parts of me. I want to make you feel more pleasure than you have ever felt in your life."

"And your hand does that?"

"Are you willing to trust me and find out?"

I don't even hesitate. "Yes."

He doesn't immediately reply, as if he's weighing my response, as if he's thinking about his. "I need to know that you were never abused sexually, Abbie. I need to know this really is pleasure for you, a game we play and enjoy together. Not a trigger."

That he stops in the middle of the emotions and physical push and pull between us and asks me this is everything. "Nothing is a trigger with you."

"Did he ever—"

"No. Sex wasn't his thing. He got off on fear, real fear. Not the emotional baggage kind of fear we've been talking about."

His hand loosens in my hair, flattens on my head. "I would never hurt you. If you ever want to stop, just say stop."

"You think I don't know that? I told you: I know you."

"Suddenly," he says softly. "I hope you do."

And then he's kissing me again, and somehow it's tender and rough with the demand at the same time, but then that makes sense. This is Gabe. This is the man I could fall in love with. This is the man I *am* falling in love with.

CHAPTER NINETEEN

gabe

Her submission. Her trust. *Her.* I just fucking want her. I fucking love her though I won't admit that, not now. Maybe not ever. I fold her naked body against mine and turn her, walking her toward the couch, pushing her. I am pushing her. I am pulling her closer. I'm a contradiction where she's concerned. Beyond reason, I want her to run if she's going to run. I want her to stay, no matter how much she wants to run.

I kiss her, nip her lip again, and when she moans, I turn her, pressing her knees into the cushion, her beautiful backside in the air. Knowing what I know now about her past, I'm stunned that she never hesitates with me. That she can be this completely naked, exposed, and *vulnerable* with me. I shouldn't even be going here with her. I know what her ex did to her. I know that even if it wasn't sexual, he played power games with her. And this, this that we're doing right now, is all about power.

Her power.

She has the power to make me want to please her. To make me need her. Only is that really what I'm doing right now? *Fuck.* No. This doesn't feel right. I step to her, pull her up and around and then I'm sitting on the couch, pulling her into my lap, her hips straddling my hips. "Come here," I say, tangling my fingers in her hair and pulling her mouth to mine.

"What happened to spanking me?" She presses against my chest. "Don't let my past be here with us now. Please. You spanked me once before. I was fine then, I'm fine now."

"It's not about fear. It's not about him. It's about being able to do this." I drag her mouth to mine, capture her lips with a soft tease of a touch. "And this," I say, this time licking past her teeth, a slide, a stroke, a tease that becomes a full-on hot, hungry kiss.

We ignite and it's nothing gentle. She dives fingers into my hair, sinking in low and deep, her breasts nestling my chest. The low and deep I need is inside her and I lift her, pressing inside her, and holy fuck, she's hot and tight. I pull her down, oh yes, this time I'm pulling, and she moans a soft little sexy sound all the way down my cock. "This is what I needed," I say, sliding back and forth inside her and cupping her backside to pull her forward. "But I can still spank you just fine like this." My hand comes down on her backside and she gasps and gives a little, "Oh", followed by exactly what a good hand palm intends.

She arches into me, clenches around my cock and I drag her mouth to mine again, thrusting into her at the same time. She moans and grabs a handful of my hair, giving it a rough tug. I cup her backside again, the only warning I'm giving her before I smack one cheek again, this time harder. She arches into me again, tugs harder on my hair. I spank her again, and our frenzied rush of hard thrusts and grinds, becomes a frenzied hot burn that has me rolling her to her back; driving deeper, harder, faster.

Her pants and a cry of my name is what undoes me. That and the lift of her hips, and tight clench of her sudden orgasm, sex, and holy fuck, I'm over the edge. I shudder, like I haven't shuddered in years, a full body, mother of God of explosion I swear to the same God I feel from my balls to my damn toes.

HER SUBMISSION

This woman owns me. That's all I can think, as we collapse into each other and I roll us to our sides, tangling our limbs because I just don't have it in me to get up right now. "Holy hell, woman," I murmur, cupping her face. "No more push and pull. I'm just going to keep you right here with me."

She laughs. "Says the man that just had an orgasm and spanked me."

I lift up on my elbow, spy my shirt, and snag it for her. "About that spanking," I say, pressing the cotton between her legs. "You still didn't a real spanking."

"My backside would argue that point," she laughs. "It stings, thank you very much."

"And stings is good or bad?"

She splays fingers on my cheek and kisses me. "I liked it, and you know it. And you liked it, too."

"Hmm. Indeed. I liked the fuck out of it."

Offering me a coy smile, she sits up, holding up my shirt. "No condom needed, right?" Her back is to me which somehow only makes that comment ten times more impactful.

She tries to stand and I catch her wrist, throwing my legs off the side of the couch to sit next to her. "Abbie," I say softly, a plea that she let this go, at least for now.

She turns to face me, naked as the day she was born, but she doesn't seem to care. I sure as hell don't. "What made you need that finality?"

I don't ask what she's talking about. The condom comment was the prelude to the expected. And I get it. I've shut her out, and if tonight taught me anything, it's that I can't keep asking her for more, and not giving it back. And yet, somehow, I'm still not ready. Not for this. "I hate condoms," I say, standing up and pull her to her feet. "Let's order dinner. You can ask me questions then."

"Just not about that."

"Anything *but* that."

"Or Kendall."

Same topic, but I don't say that. A muscle in my jaw ticks. "Or Kendall."

"Let's make a list of the topics to avoid over dinner. No KM. That would be Kendall, your ex-girlfriend. And absolutely no vasectomy talk. No baby talk, even if it's not about me and you and babies, because of course, we can't have babies." Her cheeks burn red. "Forget I just said that." She twists out of my arms. "I should leave."

For once, I should let her leave, because if I don't, we're going to talk about babies. And the last fucking thing I want to talk about is babies. Because babies lead to Kendall.

CHAPTER TWENTY

gabe

Abbie darts away from me and reaches for her clothes. I pull on my sweats, and shove a rough hand through my hair, and of course, she must think I hate babies. I don't hate babies. I love fucking babies with those chubby cheeks that explode with giggles. They're kind. They're funny. Bad for them is flinging a shit filled diaper, and that mess, I can clean up. Others, I can't. I just don't want to have babies. I don't want to talk about why I don't want to have babies. Except, fuck me. Don't I want everything I can get with Abbie?

She's already pulling her shirt over her head, already back in her legging things she wears. She's going to leave if I let her. I'm not going to let her. I catch her arm and pull her to me. "I'm a dickhead. I'm an asshole. I'm a fucked-in-the-head dickhead asshole with a closet of demons that I don't want to eat you up like they do me. But I'm crazy about you, Abbie. Please don't go."

"You're confusing me, Gabe," she says, her fingers pressed to my chest, all soft and sweet and perfect in every way. When she touches me, I'm alive, I'm a different man. I'm a different person. I want things I shouldn't want, things I can't help but want with this woman.

"I get it. I do. But just know this. I wouldn't be anywhere else right now, with anyone else. I want everything with you."

"Everything?" she laughs bitterly. "We know that's not true. We can't even talk about babies or KM."

I scrub my jaw and look away, inhaling with bad memories that want to surface.

"Never mind," she says. "Let's—I want to go home."

I curse under my breath and shackle her waist. "Time, baby. I need time. I'm not shutting you out. I just need time. Can you give me that?"

She stares at me for several long beats and then her expression softens. "I'm trying. I have my own demons. They're about trust and transparency. You know that."

"I do and that's why, pretty soon, I'll be spread wide, like a dog wanting a belly rub."

She laughs, a soft, sweet laugh that calms even all those the sharp edges of my past. "Is that a promise?"

"It is absolutely a promise. Do you know what you should do when there are two people with demons of the past in the same room?"

Her brow furrows. "No. What?"

"Eat pizza and drink wine. I say we try it and if that doesn't work. We try another spanking." I'm rewarded with more of her laughter. "I take that as an agreement on all suggestions. Hell, let's be crazy and watch TV together." I soften my voice and stroke her cheek. "Let's just slow down and be together. Can we do that?"

"Yes," she agrees softly. "I'd like that.

A few minutes later, we've taken Dexter out, and are now settled in the living room on the couch, with the pooch at our feet, begging for love. Abbie obliges and while she gives him love, we talk through the what and where of the pizza order, I fill wine glasses with a red blend, and we settle in to pick a movie. We end up with Game of Thrones instead, which we both discover neither of us has ever watched.

"Virgins together," I tease.

She laughs. "Yes, well, virgins at something."

I'm damn sure a virgin at whatever this is going on with her. I set-up the show to be ready to start when the pizza arrives and despite Dexter's efforts to get between us, I nudge him back down and scoot close to her, our thighs pressed together. He then proceeds to knock over my wine which goes all over my shirt.

I let him off the hook because the damn dog was in a cage, deserted by his former family, and he gets to milk that shit a long damn time. I yank off the basic white tee and clean up the mess.

Once we settle back down to watch our show, Abbie is watching me. Her hand closes over the tattoo on my arm, her touch radiating through me, and suddenly, I could give two shits about pizza and TV.

"Faith and strength," she says, repeating what I'd told her it means to me. "Things that remind you of your mother."

I cover her hand where it rests on my arm. "Yes. Faith and strength. It reminds me that I need to be the man she wanted me to be."

"But you don't think you are that man."

"Not as often as I'd like to be, but you remind me why I should be those things, that man. You remind me of all the things I once wanted."

"Until something happened that changed you."

"Yes. Until something happened that changed me."

"It was bad?"

"It was—fuck, yeah, it was bad, Abbie, but you know bad. I know you get it."

She inhales and lets it out. "What I admitted—about my ex, about what he did to me—Gabe, I know it makes me pressure you, it makes me struggle with trust. I just want to say that I know that's not fair to you. I know what happened earlier wasn't just about you. It was about me. It was about him."

I lean in and kiss her, my hand at the back of her head. "I will remind you that I'm not him until you don't need to be reminded anymore. And you—"

"And I'll remind you that I'm not her until you don't need to be reminded anymore."

I don't tell her that I'll have to be reminded for the rest of my life. I damn sure don't tell her that Kendall is the one person who might have the power to destroy us. The way I destroyed her.

CHAPTER TWENTY-ONE

abbie

Gabe and I eat pizza, binge-watch three episodes of Game of Thrones, and then I end up in a hot bath while he walks Dexter. They arrive back in a burst of energy, with Dexter all but leaping into the tub, and I'm officially laughing. I laugh a lot with these two but there are a few perfectly surreal moments. The first happens as I'm drying off and pulling on one of Gabe's T-shirts, while he and Dexter are roughhousing on the bathroom floor, making my efforts near impossible. I scold them and I'm immediately pulled into the battle.

The next surreal moment is when Gabe pulls me into bed, my head on his shoulder, holding me close, my body cocooned in blankets and him. It's the kind of perfection I've never known with a man. I didn't think I'd ever even go to bed with another man after my divorce, let alone find it this perfect.

The third surreal moment is directly after the second, when Dexter jumps on the end of the bed. Smart boy that he is, he doesn't crowd us, but rather, takes a corner. Gabe lifts his head and glances at Dexter. "Smooth operator for a serial killer, isn't he?"

I laugh. "Yes, he is."

He strokes my hair. "You're coming to work with me tomorrow." It's not a question, and he doesn't stop there.

"I'll set you up with Human Resources. We'll get you started on a new career."

Surreal moment over, I inch up to my elbow to look at him. "I need to be at the shelter with my mother."

"Your mother needs to stay away from the shelter. There are no animals there. Grab your phone. Text her and tell her to come to my office tomorrow."

"Your office?" I ask, rolling over and grabbing my phone before sitting up. "You think she should come to your office? And even if she did, which she won't, isn't that disruptive to your staff?"

"She can stay with the new boyfriend. Just keep her out of the spotlight."

"Boyfriend? Oh god. She does have a boyfriend. Why do I feel so weird about that? She's a grown woman. A beautiful woman. She never dates. I should be happy for her."

He raises up on his elbow. "You're not happy for her?"

"I am. *I am.*"

"Two I ams. That means you aren't."

"No, I am."

"Three I ams," he teases. "You don't like Brandon?"

"He's fine. I barely know him."

"Then what's the problem?"

"I'm protective, I guess. I'm projecting my history on her, I think. I don't want her to get burned."

"And yet here you are with me." His voice softens. "I'm going to burn you, Abbie."

"Not on purpose." I punch in my mother's number.

"Not on purpose?" he asks.

"It's ringing," I say dodging that ball. "Abigail?" my mother greets groggily. "Is everything okay?"

"Yes," I say. "Of course. Everything is fine."

"Are you sure? It's midnight."

"Oh right." I glance at the clock and Gabe. "It's midnight. Sorry. I just want you to keep a low profile tomorrow. What's your plan?"

"I'm staying with Brandon. I'm going to stay here until the police interview and go from there."

"Right. Good." I turn away from Gabe, irritated at myself for being weird about this thing with my mother. She deserves a relationship. "He's taking good care of you?"

"Yes, honey, and I'm taking good care of him. What about you? How are things with Gabe?"

"Gabe's wonderful," I say and Gabe chimes in.

"And very sexy!" he calls out.

My mother laughs. "He's quite the character."

"Yes, he is," I agree, poking him and when he lays down, I do the same. "He's the reason we have Reese Summer on our side."

"I know that. He's a good man. I hate he's gotten wrapped up in this." She's quiet a moment. "He's very into you very quickly."

My brow furrows. "What are you implying?"

"He wouldn't—he didn't—"

I launch into a sitting position again, knowing where she's going and on the phone of all places. "Don't even finish that sentence," I say, appalled that she would think Gabe killed Kenneth. "Please. Because I don't want to get angry with you." The words snap from my mouth and Gabe's hand comes down on my leg. He's willing me to look at him but I can't. Not when my mother just suggested he did this.

"I really can't believe you were going to go there," I say, my voice low, but even to my own ears, it still manages to whip and burn. Dexter belly-crawls to lay in front of me, his head tilting as if he's contemplating how badly I need a tongue bath.

"Well, for the record," she says, "I wasn't talking down about him. If he did it, which I know he didn't, he would have been my hero."

"My god, mother. How can you say that? A man is dead."

"Kenneth was a bastard. He hurt you. We both know he hurt you in all kinds of horrific ways."

I squeeze my eyes shut. "I dealt with it."

"Did you? I don't think you did. I still don't think you have."

"He would have hurt you," I remind her.

"To hurt you. It was always about hurting you, Abigail. Enough. Enough about that man. Get some rest. We can talk about this when this is over because Reese assured me it would be soon. I love you."

I exhale a breath lodged in my throat. "I love you, too."

"Tell Gabe hi for me, honey. Goodnight." She hangs up.

I set the phone on the nightstand. Gabe eases Dexter back out of my space and then pulls me down on the bed to face him, his hand settling on my face. "What just happened?"

"She thinks you did this and she thinks that makes you a hero."

He studies me for several long beats. "She watched bad things happen to you. That's not easy when it's someone you love."

"You don't wish death on people, though. That's not right. That's not the way to handle anything."

"Right," he says and it's like a wall slams down between us. "You're absolutely fucking right." He sits up, giving me his back, shutting me out.

Stunned, it takes me a moment to process but I'm certain I've hit more than one nerve, perhaps more than one demon of his past. Scrambling to my knees, I quickly follow him, settling on my knees beside him, facing him, my hands on his arm. "What just happened?"

"What would you do if you felt someone was threatening the life of your mother?" He looks at me, his eyes deep pools of blue torment. "What would you do to protect that person?"

"Anything," I say softly. "Gabe, what are you telling me?"

"You want to know who I am? You want honesty?"

"Yes. You know I do."

He runs a hand over the muscles at the back of his neck. "A few months back, a pregnant woman showed up and said her baby belonged to Reese."

I blanch. "What? No. Tell me no. He and your sister seem so perfect together."

"They are. It was a scam. That's what you heard Reid talking to me about at Cat's place. The entire thing was a set-up, a money grab. The father of the woman's child was an attorney who hates Reese. Long story short, he was stalking Cat. He was crazy. He was a fucking lunatic. He was also a gambler who owed money to a bookie."

I blink, not sure where this is going. "And that connects how?"

"I called and told the bookie where to find him. He, in turn, ended up in the hospital, where he couldn't hurt my sister anymore." He stands up, his hands settling on his hips, over the waist of his pajama bottoms. "I don't feel guilty. He was a bad person. He could have attacked or killed my sister. She was a mess. She could have lost the baby. It was destroying her and Reese. So, that's what I would do to protect someone I love. As you said: anything. Not even Reid knows for sure that I did this. He suspects, but I never admitted it. Now you and I know. And if that makes me like your ex, if that makes me someone you can't live with, I need to know now."

CHAPTER TWENTY-TWO

gabe

I stand there staring at Abbie as she sits on her knees on my bed, my T-shirt clinging to all of her soft curves, the way my body had been a few minutes ago. The way I want to hold her again, but I don't know if I ever will. I had no choice but to make that confession. If she's going to end up hating me, if that's where this ends, it needs to end now. Because if she can't handle this, she can't handle what happened with Kendall.

She scoots to the edge of the bed and stands up, walking toward me, stopping a lean from touching me. "What happened to him? The man you handed over to the bookies."

"He survived," I say. "But he could have died. I was clear on that point when I handed him over, but it was *him* or my sister and her unborn child. I chose my sister and that baby."

"There was no other way?"

"We tried. Walker Security tried. The problem was layered and complicated and time wasn't on our side."

She studies me for a few more beats, but still, she doesn't touch me and I don't touch her. Why would I touch her if she hates me now?

"No one else knows this?" she confirms.

"No, Abbie. No one else knows this."

"You trusted me with this information? Or you're using it to try to push me away."

"Both," I admit. "If you can be pushed away, you should walk away sooner rather than later. I don't want to be all in and you're toeing your path with me."

Suddenly, she's stepping to me, her arms wrapping my waist, her chin tilting upward, her eyes meeting mine. "I'm not toeing anything with you. You're not like Kenneth. He hurt people to help himself. You were just protecting your sister."

"You say that now, but—"

"I'm not going to change my mind and you have no idea how much it means to me that you trusted me with this. My God, Gabe. It's honest. Honest is what I want. Honest is what I want us to be. This means everything to me."

I cup her head and lower my forehead to hers. "Don't change your mind."

"I'm not going to change my mind."

I pull back to look at her. "If you do come to work for us, and I hope you do, you need to know that in business—"

"You're brutal. You play to win. Gabe, it's business. It's what you need your attorney to be when you hire one. I'm not naïve. And I hate that you put yourself in the same space as my ex. There is no comparison."

"You compare me to him."

"You're right. You *are right,* and I'm wrong to do that. You aren't him."

"Are you sure about that?"

"Are you going to corner me in a closet and beat me while you rip my clothes off, Gabe? Are you going to tell me someone is dead, and you did it, and I'm next while beating me?"

I go cold inside, pure ice. "Holy fuck. If he was alive, I'd kill him." I cup her face. "I spanked you. My God, I spanked you. Abbie, I'm sorry. I—"

"You asked me first. It's not the same. I liked it." Her hand flattens on my chest. "Me telling you what he did to me—that was me trusting you like you trusted me. Don't turn me into a delicate flower and make it backfire on me. If you do that—"

"No delicate flower," I say. "Got it. And you want to be spanked again, sooner than later."

"You're ad libbing."

"Very well, I might add."

She laughs and I kiss her, because I can't not kiss her, that's what she does to me. And when the kiss ends, it's not really over, but rather a pause, waiting for more. Because nothing is ever enough with this woman. "I'm going to fall in love with you, Abbie. Then what?"

Her eyes soften. "We aren't going to fall in love, remember?"

"And if we do?"

"I don't know how to be in love, Gabe."

"Maybe there's a good how-to book online." I wink. "I'll get on Amazon tomorrow."

She gives me a small smile and I drag her back to bed with me, turning down the lights and holding her close, her head settling on my shoulder. "We'll be afraid together. Just don't let me fall in love alone."

"I'm not going to fall in love with you, Gabe," she whispers. "You're not going to fall in love with me, either."

I smile because, one: she says those words with all kinds of love in her voice, and two: I've learned that with Abbie, she says we're not when we are. And we are. We're falling in love and yes, it's scary as fuck, but so is bungee jumping and I did that once. It was a dare with no endgame. Now, I have an endgame. Abbie in my bed over, and over, and over again. Every single night.

Morning comes far too soon with Abbie curled to my side but duty calls, as in Dexter, who is whining beside the bed. I sneak out of bed and Abbie snuggles into the pillow deeper, still asleep. To me, this is about comfort and trust and it matters. It matters a whole hell of a lot especially under the circumstances she's living right now and has lived in the past.

I sneak into the bathroom, throw on sweats and a tee, and quickly brush my teeth. Dexter waits impatiently and the two of us head downstairs. We've barely made it to his pee spot at the corner when I'm accosted by damn reporters. Apparently, the news of Kenneth's murder has led back to my doorstep. I keep my head down and dodge questions while Dexter does his best serial killer impression for one particularly rude man. That's my cue to pick up the pace. I run Dexter down a side street and escape. New dog parent problem. I'm going to have to hire a dog nanny just to avoid the press.

Once we're back at our building where we repeat the hell of being accosted again, but escape quickly with the help of the building staff. Dexter and I tip well with cash and doggy kisses, and we head upstairs. Once we're there, I feed him, and while he eats, I make coffee and intend to wake up Abbie when Blake calls.

"I'm in hell over here, man," I say when I answer. "I can't even take my dog out to pee because of the press."

"Considering the new developments in the case, that's expected, don't you think?"

A bad feeling rushes through me. "What developments?"

My cellphone buzzes with another call. "That'll be Reese." Blake says. "He wants to meet you as soon as possible."

"What the hell is going on, Blake?"

"They have footage of the killer leaving Kenneth's house."

I stand taller. "And?"

He hits me with the bombshell details, hard and fast. I listen and remotely remember a promise to call Reese back and something about more security. We disconnect and I'm still shell-shocked, trying to process what I just heard when Abbie walks into the room, looking sexy as hell in a silk robe, her hair a mussed-up mess, her face clean, a smile on her lips. "Good morning."

Only it's not. It's really not. I now have to tell her what Blake just told me.

LISA RENEE JONES

CHAPTER TWENTY-THREE

gabe

Abbie gives me one long look and her smile fades. "What's wrong?" She hurries forward and stops on the other side of the island with Dexter making some crazy chirping sound at her side.

She's worried, really worried, but she manages to look at Dexter, cup his face and whisper, "I love you, too, boy," because apparently, dog chirping means "I love you." Who knew?

She continues to rub him and looks at me. "What's wrong?" she repeats. "Tell me before I go nuts here."

I offer her the cup of coffee I made for her. "I was just bringing you a coffee in bed. You ruined the surprise."

"Gabe," she warns. "Please. Tell me what's going on. I know you well enough at this point to read you."

A profoundly impossible statement that she's made possible. I set the cup down. "Let's go sit down."

"No. Let's not go sit down. Tell me now."

My cellphone rings and I glance at it where it rests on the island to find Reese on the caller ID again. "What does he know that I don't?" Abbie asks.

"I need to take this, baby. Give me a minute and—"

She pushes off the island and walks toward the window, which is a win, considering a few days ago she would have run for her clothes and the door. Progress, it seems, is the bright side of this morning gone wrong. She kneels to love on Dexter, letting him comfort her, and I swear my cold heart warms.

I answer the call. "Reese."

"You heard?"

"Yes."

"And that one-word reply tells me that Abbie is there and doesn't know yet."

"No. She doesn't."

"Why?" Reese presses. "She needs to know."

"I've known about ten minutes, man. I need at least ten minutes and thirty seconds."

"We should meet sooner than planned. Let's have coffee. It might calm Abbie enough for her to really talk to me."

"We have the press all over us."

"You're resourceful. Meet me at the coffee shop on 15th. No one will be looking for us there."

"That's not secure enough. We'll stick to the plan. Your office."

"We're swarming with press."

"But not press intended for us and it's secure there. We need secure."

"Right. Have it your way. I'll send Walker to get you. I'm about to get on the phone with Abbie's mother."

"Does she know?"

"Not yet. That's why I'm about to get on the phone with her. More soon."

"When do you want us?" I ask.

"I have ten piles of disaster growing in my office. The sooner the better."

"An hour."

"One hour," he agrees. "Cat's joining us."

"I'm going to bring Reid."

"Expected."

We disconnect and I text Reid: *Problem. Reese's office in an hour.*

He replies with: *I have a meeting in an hour we don't want me to miss.*

I grimace and type: *Fuck the meeting.*

He answers with a quick: *WTF is going on? Call me.*

I reply with: *Call Cat. I can't talk.*

His answer is instant: *FUCK.*

Yep. That about sums it up. I slide my phone into my pocket and walk toward Abbie, who abandons Dexter to stand up but she doesn't turn to look at me. I step behind her, wrapping my arms around her.

She rotates to face me, those green eyes search mine in earnest, her expression stretched tight. "Gabe?" Her hands flatten on my chest, warm and soft, delicate and sweet. "Why do I feel fear right now?"

"The police have a video of a woman leaving your ex's apartment on the night he was murdered."

"Okay. Why is that bad? It feels like closure. Do they know who it is?"

"They called Reese, Abbie. They want to talk to you sooner than later."

"Me. Why me? I wasn't there. I was with you."

"I know that. You know that, but—"

"But what?" She pales. "She had red hair."

"Yes. She had red hair."

"It's a set-up. You know it's a set-up. I was with you. You can tell them. Right? You'll tell them."

"Easy, baby. Breathe. Yes. I'll tell them, but they could easily decide we're in on this together and that I'm covering for you."

She twists out of my arms and tries to take off. I catch her and pull her back to me. "Where are you going?"

"We can't be together. Not until this is over. And you can't tell them I was with you."

"Of course we can be together. Of course, I'm going to tell them—"

"No. No. No." She pokes my chest. "No. I'm breaking us up. I'm crazy about you, Gabe, but I won't see you anymore. Not now. Not—"

I cup her head and kiss her. She resists, holding herself stiff in my arms for several seconds until finally, she not only kisses me, she's kissing me back and doing it like it's our last fucking kiss.

"No," I say, pulling my mouth from hers. "Do not fucking kiss me goodbye. The police already know we're together. Hell, the reporters out front sure as hell do."

"What reporters?"

"We're surrounded," I say. "Obviously Kenneth's murder investigation is now fodder for the press. But fuck them. The point is, that saying anything different about us will not help us. In fact, it might hurt us. I have camera footage that I can turn over to the police. I have a security system. We can prove where we were that night."

"What if it doesn't cover the right times? What if it's when we were sleeping or at dinner or at my place?"

"Panicking does us no good."

"When do the police want to meet?"

"Reese has court this afternoon. I'm assuming this evening, maybe even at the courthouse. Go get dressed. We need to get moving."

She gives a choppy nod and I manage to get her to the bathroom. Once we're there, I turn on the hot water, strip her naked, and pull her under the water with me, wondering when she's going to have the last piece of this puzzle hit her. It doesn't happen until she steps out of the shower. She's holding a towel when she drops it. "Oh God. It wasn't me but—Gabe." She swallows hard. "You know what I'm thinking, don't you?"

"Your mother's a redhead."

CHAPTER TWENTY-FOUR

gabe

"I have to call her. I have to go see my mother." Abbie tries to pull away from me but I hold her close, folding her naked body into mine.

"Not yet. Wait, baby."

"Why not yet? No, no waiting. Let me go."

"Not yet," I repeat. "Stop and think."

"I need to know if she was there."

"One: you don't want to talk to her on the phone that can be listened in on. Two: we'll know more when we get to Reese's office. Neither Blake nor Reese wanted to tell me much for the same reason. The phone is a dangerous communication method."

"There's more to tell?"

"Nothing big or they would have warned me. They didn't."

"Gabe," she breathes out, torment in her voice. "She isn't a killer, but would she confront him? What if she *was* there? What if they blame my mother?"

"She has the best legal counsel possible in Reese and so do we."

"I'm scared."

"I know you are." I tilt her face up to mine. "I'll protect you and your mother. That's a promise. And remember what I told you last night. When I protect someone, I don't fail."

"And who protects you?"

Dexter barks and my lips curve. "Dexter, the resident serial killer."

She wraps the towel around her and leans down to hug the big pup, tension easing from her shoulders. Damn if that dog isn't earning his keep and earning it well, but right now, I'm thinking about the redhead. It's an obvious set-up. I pull Abbie to her feet. "Someone is trying to take us down, baby. We won't let them. Dress for the office. We need to make damn sure we go on with our life. We need them to know that we have nothing to worry about but they do."

Lies.

They cut like knives. They create wounds that don't just bleed, they fester. I've been cut. I'm still feeling the pain and the sense of betrayal never to become trust. But Gabe is changing this, changing me. Someone is attacking me and my mother, and yet, I trust him. I trust him so much that when he says he'll handle this, I believe him. That promise from him is what brings me down ten notches. It's what gets me through my morning routine, as does him, by my side, shaving, and casting me concerned looks and well-timed smiles.

Still, I hurry through my routine, eager for answers, and dress in a lilac dress with a cinched waist. I've just pulled a black jacket over the top when Gabe steps out of the closet in a perfectly fitted gray suit and heads to the mirror to knot his tie. I pull on my knee-high boots and step between him and the counter. "Let me."

"I don't believe I've let anyone but my mother knot my tie."

This pleases me, as does the possessiveness of his hands settling at my waist, under my jacket. "Now you have," I say.

"Did you do this for Kenneth?"

I glance up at him, aware that he's thinking of those years when I was another man's wife. "No, I didn't." *Because my ex and I didn't have intimate moments like I do with you*, I want to add, but I'm feeling rather vulnerable and exposed right now.

"Then how did you learn?" he asks.

I glance up at him, the knot frozen in my hand mid-pull. "One of the only memories I have of my father living with us was him putting on his tie in the morning." I finish the knot and pat his chest. "All done." When I would scoot away, he tightens his grip on my waist.

"How did you learn to knot a tie?"

My lashes lower and then lift. "I begged my mother to teach me to impress him."

"Did it work?"

I shake my head. "The night I was going to show him I could do it, he didn't come home."

"And the next night?"

"There was no next night. He ran off with his girlfriend." Just saying that cuts like a freshly sharpened blade.

"How did you handle that?"

"Better than you might expect because my mother didn't. She cried so much I thought the tears might kill her."

"Did you cry?"

"Yes. For my mother. Not for my father."

"And for yourself when your ex cheated?"

"No. I didn't cry for myself. I didn't cry because of him, Gabe. No man who cheats deserves my tears. I will never cry for a man like my mother cried for my father."

He studies me several thoughtful moments. "Nor should you." He speaks those words almost vehemently. "No cheater is worth anyone's tears." He kisses my forehead. "We need to leave. You finish up. I'm going to confirm the dog walker." He sets me aside and I can almost feel the wall slam down, not necessarily between us. More so around him but it's different than in the past. Like there's a door cracked and waiting on me to enter, but he isn't ready to open it just yet. And I understand. I really do understand. No one reacts the way he just reacted unless he's cheated or he's been cheated on. I'm not sure if that's guilt or pain he's hiding from. I just know that he doesn't believe I can handle it. Maybe he hasn't handled it and that's the problem. He's wounded and he's far from healed.

A few minutes later, with my purse in hand, I find him in the living room and he's not talking to the dog walker. He's standing at that window, looking out at that view he claims as his escape. The place where no one can touch him and I don't miss the fact that he's doing so alone but I'm not leaving him that way.

I waste no time joining him, and at the sound of my steps, he rotates to face me. I wrap my arms around him, tilting my chin up to look at him. "I promise you, I will not lie to you. I will not cheat on you. I will not judge you. I will not blame you. I will not—"

His fingers tangle in my hair and he drags my mouth to his. "A promise is nothing but words. Words aren't enough for me. You need to know that."

"I don't know what that means."

"Your truth, my truth, is in what we do."

He's right, of course. My ex made promises. Those promises were lies.

"One day you'll trust me and I'll trust you," he says. "It'll be a good day."

HER SUBMISSION

The doorbell rings and he strokes my hair, a tender gesture that is somehow reserved. "That will be our ride to Reese's office." He releases me and heads for the door, his front door. The other door, the one in his wall, slams shut behind him.

LISA RENEE JONES

CHAPTER TWENTY-FIVE

abbie

We exit through a side door of Gabe's building to avoid the press, and do so with the help of Adam, a tall man with wavy hair, who works for Walker Security.

It's a trouble-free effort and soon Gabe and I settle into the back of an SUV with Adam in the passenger seat and another man behind the wheel. "Kenneth had women," I say as we start moving. "Any one of them could have put a hit on him and set me up."

"Do you know who any of these women are?" Gabe asks.

"A few."

"Make a list. Give it to Reese."

I reach in my purse and start writing down names for no reason but keeping my mind busy. The list is five names long but there were more. Gabe takes it from me, stares at the names and then looks up at me. "You knew these women?"

"Yes."

I point to the names. "Secretary one. Secretary two. Client. Client. Fitness trainer."

"Yours or his?"

"Mine."

His jaw clenches and he leans over and kisses me. "This is one of those reminders where I promise you I'm not him."

I realize then that I said too much earlier. "And I'm not her," I say, saying what I should have then.

"No," he says. "You're not." He pulls me close and every ounce of tension we'd felt before leaving the apartment slides away. He's not Kenneth. I'm not Kendall. We're not them. We're us and us is good.

A few minutes later, the three of us—me, Gabe, and Adam—walk into the lobby of Reese's office to find Reid waiting on us.

"I thought you had a meeting?" Gabe asks, skipping the hello.

Reid scowls an intense scowl and still manages to look like a Ken doll, all pretty and perfect. "Like I'd read a text like the one you sent me this morning and not show up."

"I told you to call Cat."

"I did," he says, eyeing me. "Which is why I'm here."

"I wasn't there," I say, objecting to the accusation in his look. "I didn't kill him. I was with Gabe that night."

"And between the two of you, the police are going to think you're both guilty and lying."

"I have security footage to prove we're not," Gabe states.

Adam steps into our newly formed circle. "Reese is ready for you."

Reid ignores him. "The woman was a redhead." He looks at me. "Your mother—"

"Was at the shelter. I remember that night. There will be witnesses. It wasn't her."

Reid's eyes meet Gabe's and something passes between them. I don't like it and I'd say so but Adam clears his throat and Gabe tears his gaze from his brother's. We walk a long hallway and Cat meets us at the door of a conference room.

"Before you ask," Gabe says, "Abbie was with me. I have security footage to prove it. We're certain Abbie's mother was at the shelter with witnesses to prove it."

Reese hurries down the hall and joins us. "I don't have much time, Abbie. This is spiraling and I need time to talk to the police before I head to court. I need you alone for a few minutes. So let's talk quickly."

"Alone?"

Gabe glances down at me. "It's okay. I'll join you in a moment." He kisses me and I have the oddest impression that he doesn't want to be in this meeting with me.

I don't understand and I want to yank him along with me. I want to object, but there isn't time. Reese is in a rush. We enter the conference room but I still manage to hear Cat say, "Dad did this, right? He set her up?"

"More like he's setting us up," Reid snaps.

"Let's sit," Reese says, shutting the door.

I sit down at the long table and the minute Reese claims the seat across from me, I explode. "I heard. They think their father set me up?"

"They think their father kills babies and feeds them to demons," he replies, "but he may well be involved. If so, if that was his intent, he did a shit job. Blake already pulled security footage from Gabe's place. You're covered. As for your mother, Blake also got security footage from the shelter parking lot and then the ranch in the Hamptons. We'll make this go away."

"Will it be that easy? It was a redheaded woman who left Kenneth's apartment the night he died."

"Probably wearing a wig," he says. "And we know very little, but forensic reports could dispute the killer as female. It's going to depend on the details of the crime. I'll flesh it all out when I meet with the police tomorrow."

"I thought they wanted to meet me this evening, after your court hearing?"

"Thanks to Blake, I feel comfortable putting them off until after my trial. I want to be focused on just you."

"And yet you needed to talk to me alone?"

"I'm not going to represent your mother or Gabe."

I blanch. "What? Why?"

"They're targeting all of you as suspects. My job is to protect my client, even if that means creating questions about other people."

"Now I know why Gabe didn't want to be in this meeting. You protect Gabe, not me."

"That's not what he wants and my partner—"

"No. You're fired, and while you're protecting Gabe, remember the email I sent to Jean Claude. Throw me under the bus, but Gabe and my mother can't go down." I stand up and Reese follows.

"Abbie—"

"Thank you for the help, Reese. I hope to celebrate Gabe being out of this mess quickly." I turn and walk out the door.

CHAPTER TWENTY-SIX

gabe

Abbie bursts out of the doorway and I catch her arms. "Whoa. What's happening? Where are you going?"

"You told him to represent me, not you? No. No. And no. In case you didn't get that. *No.* I fired him. He's all yours. We're done."

"His partner is representing me. And his partner is damn good."

"No, Gabe. You aren't—"

"I am. Cole is just as good as Reese, which is why you're staying with Reese."

"He's your brother-in-law."

"Exactly. He's partial to me. The police know this."

"Good. They need to know."

"They also know he won't represent anyone he thinks is guilty. You need him."

"If he drops you, it looks like he thinks you're guilty."

"Damn it, Gabe," Reid snaps. "I told you, you should have fucking talked to her about this."

"Yes," Abbie says. "You should have. Why didn't you?" Her eyes go wide. "Reese thinks I'm going to be charged. Is that it?"

"No, he doesn't. Reese and I exchanged text messages about this, this morning when you were sleeping. We made this decision before—"

"You and Reese made this decision," she says flatly. "Gabe, what happened to *together*? Together does not mean just you."

"I meant to talk to you this morning but the new developments were overwhelming you."

"I wasn't overwhelmed. I was shocked, as anyone would be in this situation. Don't make me seem like I'm a delicate flower. You didn't even warn me before I walked in the door."

I scrub my jaw. "I needed to talk to Reid and Cat, and Reese is in a rush. I thought you'd hear about it from Reese and it would make sense to you."

"I'm going to hire my own attorney."

"Because I'm not good enough?" Reese challenges from the door.

"And I'm not good enough to defend Gabe?" Cole asks, joining us, brushing the façade of lint off his blue suit. "Hell. He's not even going to be charged. Do I suck that badly?"

Abbie's gaze catches on Cole, a man who is not only a hell of an attorney, he's confident, arrogant. A friend. "You're Reese's partner?" she asks.

"Yes. And like Reese, I've never lost a case. I consider Gabe a close friend. Cat and my wife are best friends."

"We are," Cat interjects. "And Cole is Reese's best friend and partner. The attorney we're setting your mother up with is amazing as well."

"We can't divide loyalties," Reese states.

"If no one is being charged, then why would you be dividing loyalties?" Abbie challenges, but she doesn't give him time to reply. "Protect Gabe. I got him into this. Please just get him out." She turns to me. "We can't see each other until this is over."

"That doesn't help us, Abbie. We've had this conversation."

"It helps you get your head on straight and think about you and your family, not me."

"Abbie, damn it—"

"You matter to me, Gabe. You matter more than I wanted anyone to ever matter again, but that's why you can't win this argument. That's why I'm leaving and you can't stop me." She pulls away from me and when I would go after her, Cat steps in front of me.

"Let me talk to her."

"No, I don't want you to talk to her. Now step aside. I don't want to have to move my pregnant sister."

"Trust me. She needs to hear this from me, not you." She doesn't wait for my reply. She takes off running after Abbie.

I turn to follow but Reid catches my arm. "Trust Cat."

"And talk to me," Reese says, motioning me into the conference room.

"No way in hell am I sitting down when she's running away."

"Then stand," Reese says, "but get your ass into the conference room. I don't have a lot of time here."

I grimace and walk into the damn conference room with Reid and Cole on my heels. "I'm your new counsel," Cole states, "and you and I need some one-on-one time, but Reese needs us to multitask."

"Obviously, Abbie's being set up," I say, scrubbing my jaw. "She needs you more than I do. I can't do this now. I have to go after her."

"Trust my wife and your sister to get her back," Reese says. "Have you forgotten how resourceful and convincing she can be?"

"She and Abbie barely know each other," I argue.

"They connect," Reese says. "That's obvious."

"Agreed," Cole chimes in, all of us stepping around the conference table, but no one sits down.

Reese leans on the table. "Focus, Gabe. We're on her team. We're the ones who will get her out of this and she needs help. We can still work on her case, without her here."

"And I'm one hundred percent on board," Cole adds. "Jim, our new partner, will take over Abbie's mom's case. They're communicating. He's in trial today, but like me, he's been brought up to date on all the details."

"And those details are what?" I ask. "What don't I know?"

"Blake is certain that was a wig on the security footage, and he's not even sure it was a woman wearing it. He's working on picking up footage from adjoining locations that might connect the dots. If we're lucky, we won't need to go through any interviews. Blake will end this for Abbie and her mother."

"I can read between the lines," I say. "If it was a man in the wig, that man could be me."

CHAPTER TWENTY-SEVEN

abbie

"Abbie!"

I've just stepped on the elevator when Cat appears in the doorway and joins me. "Thank goodness. I was afraid I missed you." She settles her hand on her belly. "I'm not as fast as I used to be right now."

"I like you, Cat," I say, as the elevator doors close. "I sincerely like you. I'd love to get to know you, but I'm not changing my mind about what just happened in that conference room."

She turns me to face her. "You came to Gabe for help."

"I was going to Reid for help. To hire him. Gabe and I crossed paths unexpectedly."

"Because it was meant to be."

"Because he got unlucky. Wrong time, wrong place."

"Abbie—"

The elevator stops and a cluster of people shove their way inside, forcing us into a corner together. Cat casts me a dismayed look, clearly wanting to continue the conversation, but not about to do so with an audience. Kudos to her for good judgment. This isn't something any of us want spread around. We stand there, two sardines in a can of a dozen while she, no doubt, thinks about how to change my mind, and I think about how to let her down easy. She's Gabe's sister. She loves him. One of the things I like about her. It's also one of the reasons she should understand where I'm coming from.

The elevator dings at the lobby level and Cat and I allow the crowd to exit before we do the same. "Let's go next door and get coffee," she suggests, clearly having decided on a strategy that involves me committing to a sit-down conversation. Smart.

"I need to talk to my mother."

"Call her, after you talk to me. Abbie. *Please.* Sit down and talk to me."

"Cat—"

"If you won't sit, I'll go with you. Where are we going?"

I sigh. "You aren't going to let me off the hook, are you?"

"No, I'm not."

"Where's the coffee shop?"

"Next door. We need to watch for the press, though. We just left our security behind. Let's take the side door."

She motions me to the right and we start walking. A few minutes later, we're at a table with drinks in hand, both of us splurging on a sugar cookie as well. "I need this," I say, taking a bite with loads of icing.

"I don't," Cat says. "I'm reigning in the eating, but I've been pretty good. A little treat shouldn't hurt too much. I'm just trying to keep the dieting hell after birth to as short as possible."

"Gabe's looking forward to being an uncle," I say, reminded now of his comments.

She sits up straighter, leaning in closer. "He talked to you about the baby and being an uncle? What did he say?"

"He hasn't said it to you?"

"No." She sighs. "Me and my brothers were at odds for a long while. I thought—I thought they had a lot of my father in them. I know better now."

The father that Gabe and Reid seem to think is capable of horrible things, and yet, Cat thought her brothers to be the same. "What changed?"

"They read the letter our mother left me. They found out what our father did to her. They found out who he really was. I think they knew. I think they just didn't want to see it, or rather, him."

"And the letter opened their eyes?"

"Oh yes. Our father cheated on her. He treated her horribly. I think they both struggle with guilt over not seeing that or how miserable she was. I think they'll both end up being wonderful fathers and husbands, Abbie. They won't be like him. Gabe isn't like him. He's the reason Reid opened his eyes. Gabe—Gabe was easy to turn around. That letter undid him and put him back together. It made him a new man."

Obviously, she doesn't know that Gabe doesn't want children. I consider what she's shared about this letter, about his father cheating on his mother, and I feel as if there's a connection there I'm missing. Maybe Gabe's decision to have a vasectomy was about his father, about a fear he's like him, his children would be like him, but it feels like there's more. Whatever the case, Cat is hungry for Gabe's involvement with the baby and I feed that hunger.

"I can't speak of the past, Cat," I say, "but I can speak of now. Gabe's excited about your baby. He's happy to be in your life."

"He's happy to have *you* in his life, too, Abbie. You need to let us help you. You're family now." She leans closer again. "He's in love with you. You're in love with him. Why are we in this coffee shop instead of with him?"

"I'm trying to do what's right."

"If anything happens to you, it will destroy him. He doesn't let himself get close to people, Abbie. He did with you. Let Reese do what Reese does. I'm proud of how damn good he is. Let him do it."

"Don't you see? It's because I care about Gabe that I can't let him get hurt. That's why I need him to focus on himself and his family. I need him to come out of this on top."

"You leaving. That's the kind of hurt he won't recover from. I know my brother. If something happens to you, he will not be okay ever again. I know that's a lot to put on you, but I can't just let you walk away. Not for the wrong reasons. Get your purse and I'll get mine. Let's go back."

"I need to think."

"No. I reject that statement. You don't have time to think. Come back and talk to Reese before he has to go to court. If you think Gabe will focus on Reese when you're gone, you're wrong. Your heart is in the right place, but you're still wrong. Coming back with me is the right move."

Suddenly, I know she's right. Gabe is stubborn. He won't protect himself. I have to be there to make sure he does. "Let's go back." I stand up and she pops to her feet.

"Good decision," she says, and we waste no time heading for the door.

We make it half a block before we're accosted by the press. We link arms and start walking through the mess and we're almost back to the building when we're pulled apart. We're more than pulled apart. Someone has my arm and is yanking me down an alleyway.

"Abbie!" At the sound of Gabe's voice, I search desperately for him, not sure how he's here, or where he's at, but I need to find him. Everything will be okay if I find Gabe but all I can see is the back of a man's head while the force of his body pulls me forward.

"Gabe!" I shout, and with blessed relief, I twist around to find him running toward me. I want nothing more than to run to him, but I can't. I'm yanked around a corner and Gabe's gone, out of sight.

LISA RENEE JONES

CHAPTER TWENTY-EIGHT

abbie

Gabe's gone. I can't see him anymore and that's all it takes to jolt me into action.

I yank the man in front of me by the hair. He stumbles with the force of my pull and in that quick of a moment, Gabe is there, pulling the man away from me and shoving him against a wall. I reach for my phone to call the police, but I don't have time to react. Adam is here, stepping in front of me, big and broad, a hand on his weapon under his jacket.

"Don't call the police," he orders. "Not yet."

I blanch and when I would defy him, he's stepping beside Gabe, and the two of them are speaking to the man. No one is shooting. No one is dying. Relief and adrenaline collide and I sink against the wall.

"Abbie!"

Cat rounds the corner and she's on full speed, spotting me and running my direction.

Her presence sets me off all over again. She and her unborn child don't need to be near this. I take off running toward her. "Get back!" I shout.

"What happened?" she pants out when I step in front of her, my hands coming down on her shoulders, her pregnant belly between us. "What happened?" she repeats, inspecting me for injury.

"I don't know," I say. "That guy just grabbed me. I have no idea what just happened."

"Thank God you're safe. I was terrified. I shouted for Adam. He was close, thank God."

Two thank God statements in one sentence. She's rattled. The truth is, so am I.

"He's a fucking reporter," Adam says, joining us right as Gabe does the same, pulling me around and into his arms, his hands on my face.

"Are you okay?" he demands, his voice fierce, his hands traveling my body, inspecting me for injury. "Tell me you're okay."

"Yes. Thank God you were here. I'm fine and thank you for saving me but don't do it again." I poke his chest, thinking about what could have happened. "You could have been killed."

"He was a reporter."

"You didn't know that and he's crazy. Clearly."

His hands move to my waist and he pulls me to him, away from the group. "If you need me, I'll be there. Don't you see that?"

I swallow hard, emotion balling in my chest. "You can't be there for me if you're dead."

"You have no idea what I felt when that man dragged you down the alley." He cups my face. "Damn it, woman." He presses his hands to the wall on either side of me. "What the hell are you doing to me? And why the fuck did you leave? Together, Abbie. Remember?"

"Yes. Do you? You forgot that today on many counts."

"I know I did and I was wrong, but damn it, don't fucking leave. Yell. Argue. Punch me if you have to, but don't leave."

Don't leave. This is a hot point of his. This is a trigger and I quickly agree. "Okay. No leaving. I will just punch you instead."

"Okay," he says, completely serious right now. "That works."

I laugh and wrap my arms around him. "You're impossibly intense right now."

"You know how to fix that?"

"How?"

"Don't leave," he growls.

"I know. *I know.*"

"And you could get naked."

"Here?" I smile.

"My office. Let's go." He takes my hand but we get nowhere fast.

"What the hell just happened?"

At the sound of Reese's voice, Gabe and I break apart and watch Reese fold Cat into his arms.

The group of us come together and Cat and I tell our story. The crowd. The reporters. The sudden yanking of me down the alley.

"Where is this asshole now?" Reese demands.

"Going back to his office to have his boss call me," Gabe says, eyeing Reese. "What do you have time for now? What's our plan?"

"I have a problem at the courthouse and I'm out of time," he says. "We've—meaning all legal counsel involved—have already called and put the interviews off, pending new evidence provided by Blake." He eyes Gabe. "Let's meet tonight just to debrief and be sure we're ready for anything."

"Where and when?" Gabe asks.

"Our place at seven Reid wants to be there. I already told him."

Cat leans over and hugs me. "I'm so sorry that just happened. Reporters can be such assholes."

"I can't believe a reporter would put his hands on a person," I murmur.

"They don't make a habit of it," Gabe says. "And they're going to regret it. I'm going to sue the paper and you can use that money for the shelter."

My heart falls all over again for this man every day about ten times. His first thought is the shelter and I'm quick to kiss his cheek, and just as quick to whisper, "No. I will not fall in love with you."

"Promise?"

I laugh and there's a lot of coordination that follows. Who gets what security protection and who's riding with who to go where. Funny thing about the next few minutes is that I'm reminded of Cat calling me family. How can it not? This crazy chaos that alternates hugging and fighting, fighting and hugging, that finally leads to me and Gabe being escorted to his office by Adam, feels like family.

CHAPTER TWENTY-NINE

gabe

The walk back to the building is short and Adam and I keep Abbie between us, out of the reach of random, psycho reporters. This whole mess has been a shit show that leaves us now needing security to go along with legal counsel. The irony of which is that none of these problems would exist if not for her ex coming after her. If not for her ex, if not for my father, I suspect we wouldn't have met.

We enter the building and leave Adam at the lobby level, to fend off any press that might follow. Abbie and I have just stepped into the elevator, when my phone buzzes with a text and I pull it out, expecting Reid but finding the dog walker, complete with a photo of Dexter shaking her hand.

"Real serial killer there," Abbie teases, glancing over my shoulder. "The dog walker might need security instead of us."

"Dexter's good at fooling everyone," I say, but I'm thinking of me, not my new furry best friend. I'm thinking about what Reid said to me earlier today, about how I hide behind jokes and laughter. There was nothing funny about what I wanted to do to that reporter for touching Abbie. "Maybe we should bring him to work with us. I bet that dog would kill for you."

"Dexter would get fat from treats and the staff would be distracted by him. Plus Dexter would tell the world we're a couple in his jabbering doggy style. Which brings me to a topic we should have addressed already. If I'm working here, no touching, kissing, or familiar stuff at work." She pushes out of my arms. "I have to earn respect. I can't do that if everyone knows we're together."

"We'll never be able to hide, Abbie."

"We will," she insists. "We have to. This matters to me. I don't want to be the girl you're banging, Gabe."

"Any girl I was just banging wouldn't be at the office with me."

"Please."

That one word undoes me. Holy hell, she undoes me. "Fine. Agreed."

She gives me a prim nod and a smile. "Thank you."

The elevator halts and she turns to face forward. I grimace, disliking this new arrangement. "I'll change your mind about this," I promise right before the doors open. I glance over at her. "In my office. With my tongue."

Her lips quirk. "Then I guess I better not go to your office."

The doors open and she exits the car. I follow, and I don't touch her, kiss her, or check out her ass as I introduce her to the staff. I do, however, coordinate her meeting with Human Resources for one hour from now. That done, I lead her not to my office, but hers. Once we're inside, I shut the door, and pull her around, pressing her against it. "This is uncalled for, Mr. Maxwell," she teases. "None of this at the office."

I cup her backside and pull her to me, about to prove her wrong, when someone knocks on the door. "You have three seconds and I'm coming in."

At the sound of my brother's voice, I pause a lean from kissing Abbie, my efforts to convince her to fuck me on her desk on hold but not for long. Grimacing while she laughs, I open the door to find Reid is standing there, his shoulder on the frame. "We should debrief after the Reese meeting."

"Come the hell in," I say, opening the door wider.

Reid pushes off the door, and joins us in Abbie's office, giving her a quick once-over. "Heard you took a chunk of that reporter's hair out."

"Did I?" Abbie asks. "I sure hope so."

Reid's lips twitch. "Try harder next time. HR is ready for you now, not later."

"In other words, get out of my own office," Abbie says. "Not too subtle there, Reid, but good try."

"Tell Carrie I tried," he says. "She won't believe you, but tell her anyway."

Abbie laughs. "Right. I'll tell her. Gallant effort." She heads for the door. "I'll find my way to Human Resources." And then she's gone, shutting Reid and I inside alone.

The two of us step to the window, our thinking positions, side by side. A window, any window really, always the place where we both overlook the city and let the superpowers flow. And we need fucking superpowers right now. "Do you think dad's behind this?" Reid asks.

"We drove him out," I say. "Of course, he's behind at least some of this. I have a good mind to just go choke the bastard out and call it done."

"But would it be done? There's more to this than meets the eye." We turn to face each other. "The question for me is," he continues, "does this all come back to that property the shelter sits on, or was that all her ex's bullshit to fuck with Abbie?"

"Walker can't find a reason her ex would want that property. I'm thinking he was fucking with her."

"Or it was a distraction to keep her eyes off something else."

I lean on the beam running down the window. "Walker is looking wide and coming up dry."

"And yet Kenneth is dead and Abbie and the shelter are at the core of this."

"We can't necessarily connect those dots," I argue. "Kenneth was a bastard with a list of enemies, Jean Claude included. And as for the red wig, Abbie was his ex. She's an easy target to place blame."

"I wouldn't put that or anything above Jean Claude. She was on his radar and that is not a place to be. Ever."

The door opens and Abbie enters again, shutting it behind her, her face pale. "Jean Claude just tried to call me. He wants to make an offer on the animal shelter."

CHAPTER THIRTY

abbie

"I'm done with this, Gabe," I say, leaning against my office door. "I just want to save you and my mom, and then get back to saving cute fluffy animals any way I can." I look at Reid, who I know needs to know I'm worth hiring. "And winning legal battles against jerks like Jean Claude."

"Fuck the assholes," Reid says. "No. That's my job. Save the animals. It's a hell of lot more fun and it's a tax write-off for us."

I swear in this moment, as silly as it is, I want to tear up. Because I know Gabe hasn't had time to talk to him about this but he replied just like Gabe. "All the more reason for me to call my mother, give her the heads up, and then take whatever Jean Claude offers. She feels like she has a lead on a new place anyway."

"Jean Claude wasn't calling you, Abbie," Reid says. "He was using you to get to me."

I blanch. "What? Why? I'm confused."

"He knows things about Jean Claude," Gabe says.

"In other words," Reid explains, "anything he can use to control me, he uses. In this case, the shelter, and my brother's love life."

My throat restricts. "Translation. He's using me to hurt you."

"Don't answer that, Reid," Gabe says tightly, his jaw set hard. "I will. Just not now."

"Now is fine," Reid says, walking to the door. "I'll leave you two to fight. I know that's how Carrie prefers we do battle. And I'll leave Jean Claude a message. He won't immediately take my call. That's how he operates. It may be tomorrow before he calls back. Come see me when you can, Gabe." In other words, alone, without me. He doesn't wait for a reply. He opens the door and leaves, shutting us back inside.

The minute it shuts, Gabe cages me against it, his hands on my waist, legs bracketing my legs. "I've asked myself over and over why you turn yourself into the monster in the room. After today, I get it. I know why. Because your prick of an ex turned you into that monster. He made you take the blame for everything. He conditioned you to believe that everything was your fault. So you run, to save everyone from yourself. I'm not him. So yes, you were right. You're being used. Your ex, my father, Jean Claude—all pieces of shit—use people as weapons. We don't blame ourselves for their actions. We blame ourselves for our own actions, and blaming ourselves is an action, Abbie."

I'm stunned into silence. He's right. Kenneth messed with my head, my self-esteem. My self-worth. I do blame me all the time.

"We won't let them use us, Abbie, but they did us a favor. We found each other. We found Dexter."

My heart swells with those words. "I don't want them to take you, or Dexter, away."

"You underestimate me if you think anyone is taking me from you or you from me. He inhales and presses his hands to the wall on either side of me, lifting his body from mine. "What I want you to remember, Abbie," he adds, his voice low, rough, "is that I don't hurt people just to hurt them but when someone tries to hurt me or someone I love, I draw blood. That's who I am. That's *what* I am."

"One day you will stop talking in code and hiding who you are."

"I just told you who I am."

"Is that what that was?"

"You want more?"

"KM, Gabe. Every time you make a statement like the one you just made, she's in the room."

"Kendall was my past, Abbie. She's nothing. Now, stop blaming yourself. That's an order."

"Okay. I'll stop blaming myself, but promise me—"

"Anything you want, Abbie."

LISA RENEE JONES

CHAPTER THIRTY-ONE

gabe

"Anything?" Abbie asks.

"Anything? What do you want? An orgasm? Another puppy? A cat?"

"Now you're just trying to distract me."

She's right. I am. Distract her the hell away from the topic of Kendall and a confession that won't go my way. That's the problem. She thinks I'm a better man than I am even when I tell her that I'm not. Over and over, I tell her. I warn her. She sees something better in me than I see. She makes me want to be that better man. And I will be. That's what matters.

"What do you want me to promise?" I ask, still pressing her against her office door, holding her here. Wishing like hell I could whisk her away, deal with this problem, and then bring her back where I plan to keep her by my side. The police complicate that desire, burn it to ruins, in fact.

Her hands touch my face, fingers trail my jaw. "Promises later but food now would be good."

Aware that she's let me dodge a bullet, I take the out. "Promises in bed tonight. Lunch now. Let's order in." I push off the door. We'll move to my office and eat there, while you reach out to your mother. When do you have to be back with Human Resources?"

"One o'clock," she says. "And me in your office is pretty much announcing we're together, right?"

"I have lunch meetings all the time, baby." I open the door. "Meet me there in five, if it makes you feel better." I disappear out of the door.

I've just entered my office and sat down and she's already there. "Shut the door."

She shuts the door. "You're sure about this?"

"Yes." I motion to the conference table. "My lunch meeting location," I say, grabbing the phone and dialing Connie, Reid's assistant, who is currently covering for Lulu while she's on vacation.

Reid pokes his head in the door. "Jean Claude called. I'm going to meet him."

"What happened to a few days?" Abbie asks, twisting around to look at him.

"I'll answer that question when I get back," Reid replies, giving me a grim look, before disappearing into the hallway.

"Are you worried?" Abbie asks. "Jean Claude is dangerous, right?"

"Dead men don't do favors," I say. "Jean Claude wants a favor from Reid. That's obvious."

"Jean Claude doesn't like that Reid knows his secrets."

"He can handle himself, baby. I promise."

"Taking lunch orders," Connie announces, rushing into the office and said lunch orders turn into girl chat between her and Abbie while I end up on a call with a client. By the time our food arrives, Abbie's tried to reach her mother with no success several times. "She's acting strange since all this started," Abbie worries when we finally sit down to eat.

"In what way?"

"She never skips my calls."

"Skips your calls? Baby, I think it's more that she has her hands full."

"With what? The animals are on the island. She's here. Do you know what time she gets here for her meeting with her attorney?"

"I don't, but most likely at the same time we're meeting with Reese."

"I haven't even talked to her about her new attorney. It makes no sense. She worries about me, Gabe, and yet she's not even talking to me?"

"Relax, Abbie, baby," I say, finishing off my sandwich and tossing the wrapper in the bag. "She's fine. I'm sure of it."

It's in that moment that her cell vibrates on the table. "It's her," she announces grabbing her phone and to my surprise, answering it on speaker. "Mom, I'm here with Gabe."

"Hi, you two. Listen, I'm on my way back to the island. Gabbie has had some bleeding complications since birthing her pups and we have two other sick animals. I can't stay here. I know they want me to meet the police and another attorney, but I have to put the animals first."

"Oh God," Abbie says. "How bad is the bleeding?"

"I'm not sure," her mother says. "These situations are hard to read from a distance. Brandon has a vet going over there, but I'd just feel better if I saw Gabbie myself." She laughs. "Gabbie. Gabe. Abbie. It's kind of cute. Maybe you two should adopt her after I save her."

"So Dexter can kill her?" I joke. "I don't think so." Though a family of dogs and Abbie sits far better than I could have ever imagined. "Take care of Gabbie," I add. "We can arrange a video chat with your new attorney."

"Really? That's wonderful. Abigail, honey, I was on my way to check on you when this all went to hell. Where are you? Can you come?"

"She needs to stay," I say. "There's too much heat on you both for you to leave town simultaneously."

"By heat, you mean the redhead seen leaving the scene of the crime," her mother says. "I heard. I swear that man staged his own death and set us up. He's that evil. How are you handling this, Abigail?"

"I'm fine." Abbie's eyes meet mine. "Thanks to Gabe and his family."

"Indeed," she says. "You found yourself a real hero there. I just don't want you getting hurt in this, Gabe." There are voices in the background. "We're at the airport. I'll call you when I get back to the Hamptons and know more about Gabbie."

"Wait," Abbie says quickly. "The shelter—"

"We'll talk later, but I have a lead on a new location." She doesn't wait for a reply. "I'll tell you more later." She hangs up.

I lean over and kiss Abbie. "See? She's fine. All is well. Eat your lunch, unless you'd rather get naked and let me fuck you in my office." Connie buzzes in. "The president of First Nation United Bank is on the line and he's freaking out, throwing a fit worthy of a two-year-old that didn't get his cookie. And that is not an exaggeration."

I sigh. "So much for fucking in my office." I kiss Abbie, licking into her mouth. "But we will and soon. That's a promise and you didn't have to wait until tonight for it."

She laughs, her face lighting up, tension easing from her petite shoulders. That's what I want. Her relaxing. Her happy. Her naked in my office. Her legs wrapped around my shoulders. My mouth between her legs. Goals. I have many where Abbie is concerned.

The afternoon is not as slow as one might think, ticking by with agony and fear. It's busy, so busy there's no time for fear. I'm taught about the company's rules and policies on EEOC, workers compensation, and of course, sexual harassment. I almost laugh as the head of HR talks about inappropriate touching considering Gabe had wished me good luck this afternoon by promising to lick me in very inappropriate places as soon as humanly possible, "You're mine," he'd declared, "and I'll make you say it tonight, in bed, right before you come on my tongue."

"Good luck with that," I'd teased as I'd walked to his door but considering the clench of my sex, and the slick heat on my thighs, his victory was fairly certain.

I am his, I think as we sit in the back of a Walker Security driven vehicle, on our way to meet Reese and Cat, his hand on my knee, just under my skirt. His thumb stroking back and forth, driving me wild. I'm aroused while riding to a destination where I'll be prepping for a police interview. How is that possible? How is any of this possible? I mean, I'm being questioned regarding a murder. My ex-husband's murder.

I catch Gabe's hand, halting the assault of his fingers on my body. "Nothing from Reid?"

"Not since he went to meet with Jean Claude."

"Hours ago, Gabe. I'm worried. Has his wife heard from him? Can you text her?"

"I'm not telling her that he met with Jean Claude."

"Because she'll worry. *I'm* worried. Aren't you? Kenneth is dead. What if—"

The SUV halts abruptly and the door on my side abruptly swings open and suddenly we are no longer alone in the backseat.

LISA RENEE JONES

CHAPTER THIRTY-TWO

gabe

I grab Abbie and pull her to me only to bring the familiar man, with long dark hair tied haphazardly at his nape into view. "Holy fuck, Blake. Warn us, would you? You know the shit we have going on right now. That doesn't make for easy riding." I ease Abbie back into her seat and the vehicle starts to move again.

Blake leans forward to look at me over the top of Abbie's lap his brown eyes intense, seeking. "Fuck, man, my Uber had a flat two blocks back." And his love of the word "fuck" unapologetic. "I have something new on the sale of the shelter I didn't want to relay by phone."

"Abbie," I say, "this is Blake Walker of Walker Security. One of the founding brothers."

"I'd say nice to meet you," Abbie breathes out, "but I'm still trying to get my heart to stop racing. Obviously, I'm much more on edge than I realized."

"Sorry about that, Abbie," Blake murmurs. "I'll be better next time."

"Please tell me there won't be a next time," she replies.

His gaze is already back to me, the apology over. The reason he's here his focus. "Jean Claude's company is quietly making offers on properties around the shelter. They're all signing a confidentiality agreement. He's planning a retail complex complete with a movie theater."

"And they need the shelter property to make it happen," Abbie assumes.

"Literally," Blake states. "I got a glimpse of the blueprints. Without the shelter, they can't make this work."

"And Kenneth promised him that he could get the shelter and get it cheap," she replies bitterly.

"That we can only assume," Blake replies.

"I need to just give them the shelter," she says. "I need this over. Done."

"It's not that simple with murder in the mix, baby," I say. "That's why Reid is with Jean Claude. He'll negotiate. He'll make sure we're all protected. He and Jean Claude speak the same language."

"That's a little scary," Abbie murmurs, and those words cut right through me. I'm not so different from my brother. A fact that perhaps kept Reid and I at arms length a chunk of our lives. We see ourselves when we see each other.

My hand falls away from Abbie's leg. "Where does my father fit into this?"

"We'll talk," Blake says. "Once we're inside your apartment."

The SUV halts and I glance out of the window. "We're supposed to be at my sister's place."

"They're run over with press, thanks to Reese's trial," Blake says. "We moved you here."

He eyes the driver. "Are we clear?"

"Clear," the driver says. "No press."

Blake opens the door and gets out, running from the truth he has to tell. No. Running from Abbie before she hears the truth he has to tell. Abbie should follow him out but she doesn't move. The minute he's out of sight, Abbie turns to me, her gaze searching my face, for some awareness of where this is headed. No place good, that's for damn sure. She just landed my brother in the same bucket with Jean

Claude, and now my father is about to be exposed as the dirt I've warned her he is and always will be.

"Gabe," she whispers.

"Let's go inside."

She hesitates, worry etched in her brow, and then reluctantly scoots across the seat to exit the vehicle. Her legs start to swing outward, and I swear it's like she's leaving to never return. I catch her wrist and pull her back, cupping her head. "Abbie." That's all I say. What the hell else can I say? My mouth crashes down on hers, hungry with demand, demand she see only the good parts of me. Demand that she stay, that she doesn't leave. Fuck. I tear my mouth from hers, our lips a breath apart with my realization. All I'm doing is demanding, forcing her to submit and that's what her ex did to her.

Horns honk and she brushes her fingers over my cheek. "He's not you. I know that."

I don't know how she knows that's where my head is, how she tasted that fear on my lips, but she did. I kiss her again and say, "Let's go inside."

She exits first and I follow. Blake stands on the sidewalk, arms folded in front of him, dark eyes pinning mine over Abbie's head. The silent message in that look nothing more than a confirmation. I don't want Abbie to hear what he has to say.

The three of us head into my building and I try to figure out how I get a minute to talk to him alone. Once we're on the elevator Blake offers me that answer. "Reese and Cat are already in your apartment and Reese is eager to get started with you, Abbie."

"Get started prepping me to be questioned on murder charges," she whispers. "How is this my life?"

The answer, I am certain, is as I've feared all along but now am about to confirm. My father. I pull her to me, hold her close, wishing like hell I didn't know this was headed to a place that might just destroy us. We enter the apartment and Dexter all but tackles us both at the door. That damn dog is so happy to have a family he's about to piss himself and I get it. Abbie makes me get it. Hell, Dexter does, too. My sister is first to greet us after Dexter and she's looking all belly and smiles. She's happy, the way I want Abbie to be happy.

Reese joins us and he's quick to focus on Abbie. "Let's get you prepped and ready so we can make this go away."

"Yes, please," Abbie says, glancing around. "Where's Cole? Is he here? What about Gabe's prep?"

"Cole and I talked this afternoon," I say. "I'm fine. I'm ready."

She rotates to face me, fixing concerned eyes on me. "You need to prep. More than me. I'm not letting you go down for me."

She's protecting me. No woman has ever cared about me beyond my money and my tongue. Cat's eyes meet mine, warm and worried. She knows what I'm thinking. She knows I can't lose Abbie. My father will not be the reason. "I'm used to this kind of thing," I say refocusing on Abbie. "It's what I do." I stroke her hair. "And you know the law. You're an attorney. Use that during the interview."

"Knowing it and using it are two different things," she says. "I haven't been practicing."

"Good thing I have," Reese offers, loosening the tie around his neck. "Come on. Let's go get busy."

"I ordered pizza," Cat says. "The baby needs pizza. And ice cream." She smiles at Reese. "Right, baby?"

"Right, sweetheart." He laughs and kisses her. "We'll get a pint or ten on the way home." He glances at us. "We're set up at the dining room table. Join us when you're ready, Abbie." He and Cat walk away.

I kiss Abbie. "Go, baby. Do this."

"Go? Where will you be?" She glances at Blake and then me and understanding fills her gaze. "You want to talk to him alone."

"Don't read into this, Abbie," I say. "We're just talking."

"I know it's about your father. I hate that you don't trust me with that information. That makes me sad." She pushes to her toes, her hand on my chest, her lips to my ear. "I hate KM and I don't even know who she is. I just know that she made you this way." She settles back on her feet. "When you're done I'd really like it if you would join us. I need you, Gabe." And with that, she turns away and starts walking, twisting me in ten different directions as she does. She doesn't want me to let her walk away. She wants me to pull her back but I can't. Not now. Not until I talk to Blake.

Because I do trust her. I trust her to be a good person. I trust that I'm not. I look at Blake and motion to a small office off the hallway. We enter the room, huddling up by the door he pulls shut

"Tell me," I say. "What sins hath my father committed now?"

"He's brokering the deal for Jean Claude now that her ex is dead. He stands to make millions off the deal."

I absorb that with hard understanding. "My father benefited from her ex-husband's death."

"Yes," Blake confirms. "He stood to benefit by a sum somewhere around ten million if not more."

In other words, my father may well have killed Abbie's ex-husband and framed her for it. How does a man come back from that with a woman?

LISA RENEE JONES

CHAPTER THIRTY-THREE

gabe

I'm still standing in my apartment office with Blake when Reid sends me a text: *Where are you? I'm stuck outside in the zoo of the press at Cat and Reese's building.*

I curse. "I forgot to tell Reid we changed locations," I say, texting him back: *We diverted to avoid the press. We're at my place.*

He calls me. "We need to talk alone," he says. "Meet me at Mac's bar down the road. Fifteen minutes?"

"I'm bringing Blake. He has something you need to hear."

"Of course he does. Bring him and his load of crap to share. I have my own." He disconnects and I shove my phone into my pocket. "Reid met with Jean Claude. Now we're meeting Reid. He wants to talk. Alone."

"That doesn't sound good."

I don't comment. My brother has a way of getting things done, much like my own way—and it's not always gentle. "We're meeting Reid to do interview prep, the end. Leave it at that. I don't want to lie to Abbie, but I need her to focus on being ready for that interview, not what we have going on."

"I get it, man," Blake confirms. "I'm married. I love my wife. Prep work isn't a lie. We're trying to solve the murder. That's the best prep work that exists."

It's not a lie, I repeat in my head, because I don't need lies adding to the shit she will eventually find out about me. It's inevitable. I know it. "I need to let Abbie know I'm leaving."

"I'll head to the door and wait for you downstairs."

I nod and follow him out of the office and down the hallway. The minute we round the corner, stepping into the living area, we find Reese, Cat, and Abbie working there, not in the dining room. Blake tucks his chin and charges a path toward the front door. The room seems to follow his movement, and I step to the chair where Abbie's sitting, with Reese and Cat to her left, side by side on the couch.

"How are things?" I ask, brushing red curls from her grass-green eyes. Such expressive, beautiful eyes.

"You tell me," she says, catching my hand. "How are things?"

Better with you in my life, I think, but I say, "Blake is knee deep in research. He's got me looking at some random data related to my father." It's not what I'd planned to say, but in this moment, it feels closer to the truth.

"What kind of data?"

"I'll let you know when I know," I say. "Stay here. Focus. We're meeting Reid at Mac's and we'll see if either of us can make heads or tails of anything Blake knows. You need to get ready for the interview."

"She does," Reese agrees. "We're just getting started. Ready, Abbie?"

She doesn't answer. She doesn't look at him. She looks at me and lowers her voice, a soft whisper, that while easily overheard is intimate in its delivery. "Is everything okay? Is this about that meeting earlier?"

"Yes," I say. "But I know nothing. I'll text you. Okay?"

"This is a good time for another promise."

"I promise." I squeeze her hand. "I hate leaving you, but I need to go and you need to focus." I lift her hand and kiss it. "I won't be long." I push to my feet and I can feel my sister's eyes on me. She's stunned by my show of affection, with good reason. Abbie's changed me. She keeps changing me.

Focused on getting back, I head for the door and I don't look back. As promised, Blake is waiting on me downstairs and one of his drivers is waiting on us. Fifteen minutes later, I'm sitting in a round corner booth with my brother and Blake, each of us slowing nursing a whiskey.

"I have good and bad news," Reid starts out. "I met with Jean Claude. He pointed out the obvious. That Abbie's ex was trying to buy the property and then ended up dead. That makes Abbie a big target for the police."

"So does a red wig and a set-up," I bite out. "And that sounds like a threat."

"It is," Reid replies. "He went on to suggest that if Abbie sells him the shelter property now, at a reasonable price, she won't look as guilty."

"Of course, he did," I say dryly. "And you said what?"

"I got him to up his offer ten percent. Any higher and it still might look like Abbie had the motivation to remove her ex from the picture to get a better offer from Jean Claude."

"Unfortunately," Blake says, "I have to agree. Any big payout makes them both look guilty. Like they colluded perhaps beyond the payout for the property. Will Abbie make the deal?"

"She'll take it," I say. "And I'll make sure the animals find a home."

"We'll make sure the animals have a home," Reid corrects. "She can make this the company's first big charity operation."

"Count Walker in as well, if you need us," Blake offers.

"And just to be transparent," Reid says, "Jean Claude offered Abbie a replacement property for the shelter. I declined. You don't want to be in debt to Jean Claude but

Abbie needs to know. He'll bring it up to her if he gets the chance."

"She wants out of this," I say. "She'll walk away."

"What about the murder?" Blake asks. "What did he have to say about who killed Abbie's ex?"

"He didn't do it," Reid says. "I believe him."

"Why?" Blake demands. "Why trust a man like that?"

Reid's jaw clenches and he cuts his stare before he looks at Blake, before he tells him what I already know. "I did legal work for that man for years. I saw how he operated. There are things he could use against me. He has no reason to lie to me. And he wouldn't kill someone by way of a hitman. He's too smart for that. He'd make it look like an accident. I know. Believe me. I know."

"Were you a part of these accidents?" Blake asks, his eyes pure steel.

"No," Reid replies. "I was with him through my father. I parted ways with him when I knew how deep the shit ran, but I'm too connected to him to cut ties completely. Bottom line," he looks between me and Blake, "he needs Abbie alive and well to look good to the police and she needs him for the same reasons. Outside of that, and pertinent in all ways, he suggested the killer might be someone close to her ex, and with a personal agenda. Perhaps someone who knew Kenneth stole from him and thought he'd be pleased that Kenneth was dead."

"And is he?" Blake asks.

"No," Reid replies. "Police attention displeases him. The question now is: who had the most to benefit from Kenneth's death."

"I told him about the development," Blake says, looking at me and then glancing at Reid. "What you don't know is that your father took over Kenneth's role in that project when he died."

"And stands to benefit ten million dollars," I add.

"I'm not surprised," Reid says. "I'd already mentally gone there. Jean Claude never said his name to me but he told me to quote 'get your fucking house in order or I will.' He went on to say that anyone who brings him legal trouble won't be around long. We have to handle our father, or he will."

I look between them. "So just to be clear. We believe that our father killed Kenneth for money?"

"Yes," Reid and Blake reply at the same time.

"And I now have to tell Abbie that my father killed her ex-husband and framed her for the murder." I scrub my jaw. "How do I make this right with her?" I ask them because asking myself has gotten me nowhere.

"By putting him in jail for the murder," Blake suggests. "That gets rid of him for Jean Claude and keeps him alive." He glances at Reid. "Is that good enough for Jean Claude?"

"It might be," Reid says. "But we'll have to prove he did the crime. I have no doubt we can get him to admit it while we record him, but that's going to punch the company in the mouth. He founded the firm. We'll be the sons of a killer. Everyone we love will be stalked by the press. Our employees will be affected. We need to all step back and think about this before we take action."

"Before I do anything, I need to tell Abbie," I say. "You *know* what she's going to think. It's inevitable. Will I be just like my father? *Am I* just like my father?" I run a hand through my hair. "Hell, maybe I even told her that I'm just like my father when I wanted to scare her off. I can't fucking remember." I look at Reid. "I needed better news than this. Why the hell didn't you bring me better news?" My voice is low and taut, my words for his ears only.

He leans closer. "You aren't going to lose Abbie. I didn't lose Carrie and I shared every dirty little secret I own."

Because Carrie loves him. Because she already loved him when our bastard father went after her and us. I stand up. "I need to think." I'm walking by the time I finish that sentence and I don't look back. I just hope like hell that's not what Abbie does when she hears just how bad, bad gets with my father, with my family. With me. Hell, because that's where this is leading. I'll have to tell her everything. Before my father tells her for me. It needs to be my story, told my way, with my explanation.

Fabulous.

Fucking fabulous.

I not only have to tell her that my father killed her ex-husband and framed her. I have to tell her about Kendall.

CHAPTER THIRTY-FOUR

gabe

I walk Battery Park without even seeing where I'm going, without feeling the cold air whipping off the ocean just beyond the rail. Without caring that I have no coat. The past plays in my head. The present plays in my head. My fucking father won't get out of my head. And Abbie. Abbie is in every part of me, rooted deep and spreading like sunshine. Light my father is determined to darken, determined to destroy. I don't know how or when, but I end up in the bar by my office, the one where I met Abbie. The one really damn close to my father's apartment. I down a fast whiskey, desperate to lessen the edge of my mood, before it's my fist in his face that does the job. And I do so while sitting at the table in the corner where Abbie was sitting the night I met her. I'm not a violent man though I am a man who believes in consequences. I've never physically touched my father and neither has Reid but maybe, just maybe, that's where we went wrong. We've never made him feel real fear, and really, does a man like that understand anything else?

I'm about to order another whiskey when my phone buzzes with a text from Abbie: *Where are you? I need you.*

Fuck.

Fuck.

Fuck.

I need her, too. What in the hell has happened to me? I now have a dog and a woman waiting on me at home. *Home.*

That word guts me. I haven't had a home since my mother died. Any place where she was at, was home. Until it wasn't. Now, home is where Abbie and Dexter wait. I'm a damn fool sitting at a bar. I'm here when I should be there with them. Instead, I'm avoiding the confessions I know have become inevitable. Because I don't want to lose the woman I know as home. I type a reply: *I'm on my way back now. Are you done with Reese?*

Yes, she replies. *They're about to leave.*

I'll be right there, I answer, but Reese's prep work feels short. Why?

I toss money on the table and I'm already walking, determined to get back to the apartment before Reese leaves, his support of Abbie's interview now in question. My future with Abbie in question as well. *You aren't going to lose, Abbie.* Reid's words come back to me. Reid who has been through this. Reid who, thanks to our father, had to tell Carrie he'd been connected to a murder our father committed. Just one of the ways our father tried to control him, by setting him up, by owning him. Or at least trying to own him.

I'm almost to the building when my phone rings. I grab it, register Cat's number and answer. "You're already done?"

"Reese has a plan, which doesn't include her answering tons of questions. Which you'd know about had you been there. What's going on?"

"I can't talk about this on the phone. I'm on my way there."

"We'll meet you in the lobby," she says. "How far out are you?"

"About two minutes." I disconnect and finish the walk, stepping into the building to find Cat and Reese standing just inside the door.

"What's going on?" Cat asks again, her hand resting on her belly just under her trench coat. The belly is what gets me. She's pregnant. She's had a lot of stress. I decide right then that I'm not telling her about dad.

"Reid met with Jean Claude. He offered Abbie a buyout and we all think she has to take it. Otherwise, it looks like she was saving the shelter by getting rid of her ex-husband."

Reese scrubs his jaw. "I don't disagree but I hate having her manipulated like that. Any chance Reid recorded that conversation?"

"No," I say. "Jean Claude's not a man to cross. We don't want to go down the rabbit hole you're about to travel. Blaming him to save her will get one of us dead."

"I hate this," Cat whispers, and fuck, *great job at saving her stress, Gabe.*

"Don't fret, little sis. Reid doesn't believe he did this. Jean Claude is on our side. He wants someone to go down for this and fast."

"What keeps him from picking you or Abbie?" Reese asks.

"It seems to me like he already did," Cat says. "He just wants her to sign over the shelter before she's arrested."

"No. This comes from Reid. Reid knows him."

"Too well," she snipes back.

"He would agree," I say. "Bottom line: I have to go up there and get Abbie to agree to sell which I don't believe will be difficult." I look at Reese. "How do you feel about things?"

"Ask me tomorrow. Right now, I have another case to deal with and that's not how I like to operate. Once it's over, Abbie has me one hundred percent. Let's hope she doesn't need me."

I hug Cat. "Don't worry. All is well."

She leans back to look at me. "Dad—"

"Go home. Feed yourself and the baby. Love your husband."

"I ate pizza," she says. "We left you some."

"Hmmm," I say, studying her belly. "I think you need to eat again. The baby's sending me subliminal messages. She wants ice cream."

"We're on the way to the store," Reese assures me, and they head for the exit, a mission to feed that baby ice cream.

I don't move. I stand there in the lobby and call Reid, updating him on what I did and didn't say to Cat. We agree to protect her where our father is concerned, the best we can for as long as we can. When we hang up I force myself to get inside the elevator. I need to see Abbie. I need to talk to her. I can save Cat from this thing with my father for now but I can't save Abbie. Not anymore.

The ride is eternal, the car suffocating, adrenaline pumping through me. *I won't lose Abbie.* With those words in my head, I step off the elevator and I realize then that I've never fought this thing with Abbie. We just happened. We fell into each other, but now, I have to see me in her eyes and it scares the shit out of me.

I reach the door and instead of going for my key, I rest my head on the wooden surface, willing my heart to calm the fuck down. This will work out. I'm falling in love. Hell, I *am* in love. I could say that. No. No, I can't say that. Not now. It'll feel poorly timed and fake. And that's not the confession I have to make this time.

I'm overthinking. I never overthink. I inhale and decide to just fucking wing it. I open the door, and the minute I do, Abbie and Dexter are running toward me. I'm home. I'm so damn home and the minute they are both by my side, I pet Dexter and then drag Abbie to me. I don't want to lose her. My intended confession is tossed aside for another. "I don't ever want to come home and not have you two here to greet me ever again. Move in with me."

CHAPTER THIRTY-FIVE

abbie

I blink, stunned by Gabe's words, not even sure I've heard him correctly. "What?"

"Move in with me. I'm not even going to try to pretend I ever want you to leave, Abbie."

My head is spinning. My heart is racing. "Gabe, if this is about protecting me—"

"It's not. I mean yes, I want to protect you, Abbie, but that's one of a million things I want with you. I need you here. Dexter needs you here."

I'm terrified he'll regret this. I'm terrified he'll hurt me when he does. "You're a protector, Gabe. I don't even think you know this about yourself, but you are. Let's decide after this is over."

"We have no idea when this will be over or even how to determine the meaning of over."

Alarmed, I pull back to look at him. "What does that mean?"

"What if they don't find the killer for six months? What if they never find the killer? When is it over? Move in with me, Abbie. Say yes. Be here with me." Dexter barks his approval, feeding off of Gabe's energy.

I want to say yes. I do. I want to just be with this man. I want it to be as perfect as it feels, but I'm terrified. This is moving so fast, too fast for me to protect myself. Too fast for him to know what he really wants. "Gabe—"

"This isn't what you want." His voice is taut, his body rippling with sudden tension. "That's what this is." He cuts his stare and then looks at me, the warmth in his eyes now gone. His look is flat. His tone flatter. "That's what I needed to know." He releases me. "That's the way to put things into perspective."

"No. No perspective. I just—Gabe. I don't want you to—"

"End of conversation, Abbie." He steps around me, and then he's gone, walking away even as I try to catch his arm.

"Gabe."

I rotate and so does Dexter. We find Gabe striding rapidly toward the bar, shrugging out of his suit jacket as he does, and I can almost feel him slipping away. I don't want him to slip away. I hurry toward him and Dexter is right there by my side, a sweet, confident, but polite boy, who knows not to intrude, but needs to be close. I catch up with Gabe as he's pouring a drink.

I don't even hesitate. I'm around the bar and grabbing his arm in two seconds flat. He doesn't even turn to face me. He fills his glass. "Please talk to me."

"I'm drinking right now."

"You aren't giving me the chance to explain."

"You explained just fine."

"Obviously I didn't or you wouldn't be angry right now."

He downs his drink and refills it. I grab the glass and take a big swig, the amber liquid burning a path down my throat, but still, Gabe doesn't look at me. "I'm scared," I admit. "You scare me."

He looks down at me. "And I'm not worth that risk, the way you are to me. Check. Got it."

"You know what I went through. You know how much I have to overcome."

"And you have no idea what I went through and you never will."

Anger flares wicked hot. "And there it is. The reason I'm so damn scared with you. You have secrets you never want me to know. Secrets some part of you has determined can't be told. Telling me destroys us. You don't trust me or us and yet you want to move in together? When you trust me, *really* trust me, then I'll move in with you." I set the glass down and turn away from him.

He catches my arm and suddenly he's facing me, dragging me to him. "I told you, I need time."

"And I respect that, but how do I move in with you now, Gabe? My God. Don't you see how hard I'm falling for you? Don't you see how easily you could hurt me? What if you never trust me? What if you never really believe in me or us?"

"Abbie, damn it—"

"I'm going to fall in love with you and you're going to break my heart. This is how this ends. I need to keep my apartment. I need a place of my own to fall when it's over."

He drags me closer, fingers tangling in my hair. "I'm not letting you fall anywhere but into me, woman. What part of that do you not understand? I'm not walking away." And then he's kissing me, a deep, curl-my-toes kiss, and I'm no longer holding back.

Sinking into his long, lean, hard perfection, he's warm and strong and I hold on tight. I never want to let go. I have never in my life wanted anyone the way I want Gabe. I have never needed anyone the way I need Gabe. I have never wanted to kiss until I can kiss no more, but I do now. I do with Gabe.

"Say you'll move in with me," he demands, tearing his mouth from mine.

"Gabe," I whisper, desperate for him to understand. "Take the time to trust me. I will give it to you."

"I trust you."

It's then that I realize that denying him anything is like holding me and us ransom and that's not what I want. That's not what I mean to do. "I want—"

"I want," he echoes and his mouth closes down on mine, and this time, there is demand and lust in his kiss, in his touch. He owns me right there by the bar, without ever taking off my clothes. This man claims me with his tongue, with his hand running down my back. With the emotions inside him, overflowing into me, around me. This man consumes me.

I don't even think about holding back when he yanks my skirt up to my waist. My sex clenches and my mouth is right there with his, colliding again, tasting the hunger on his lips as my own. He grips my panties and yanks, my yelp transforming to a moan as his fingers slide along the wet seam of my body, pressing inside me. "Gabe," I pant, gripping his tie and pulling on the knot. He has on too many clothes.

He lifts me and sets me on the counter and in a frenzy of movement, he's just naked enough to press his cock inside me, to drive into me, thick and hard. And he does. He drives deep, nestles into the farthest part of me, and whispers by my ear, "I need you with me, Abbie."

Need.

That word undoes me. He undoes me. I want to say as much but he's suddenly driving into me, sensations rocketing through me, my hips lifting into his hips; fingers gripping his shirt. I suck in a breath, intending to speak but words don't come. His thrust does. His cock drives into me and my legs wrap his hips. Over and over, he pumps, thrusts, drives, and grinds into me. Over and over, he kisses me, touches me, pleases me to the point that I can't breathe. I can't think. It's intense. It's fast. It's insanity and the best insanity I have ever known.

I come fast, too fast, but he follows, both of us quaking with release. Both of us clinging to each other. We collapse with the ease of our orgasms, his face buried in my neck. My fingers tangled in his hair and I press my cheek to his, lips at his ear as I say, "And I need to be with you," I confess.

He pulls back to look at me. "What does that mean?"

"It means I get it now. You need to know I trust you enough to take this risk. You need to know that before you trust me enough to confess what you believe to be your sins. So yes, Gabe. I'll move in with you. I would be so very happy to move in with you."

"You said—"

"That I was scared, and I am, but I get it now. You are, too. So let's be scared together."

He cups my face and stares down at me, searching my eyes, looking for truth and then saying, "Yes. Let's be scared together."

LISA RENEE JONES

CHAPTER THIRTY-SIX

gabe

I'm not going to make my intended confession to Abbie. Not now. Not this night.

I don't want the moment I asked her to move in with me to become about the past or even my father. For now, for this night, I want to revel in her calling my home her home. I want to revel in all the nights we will sit on the couch as we do now, waiting on a takeout order while ignoring the cold pizza my sister left behind. I know I need to talk to her about KM. I know I need to get it over with but Dexter starts chasing his tail, and the mood is light.

"What happened with Jean Claude?" Abbie dares, though I can tell she's hesitant to break the mood.

"He was a dick. He made an offer as you said. Reid got it up but if it's too high it looks like you had a reason to get rid of Kenneth."

"I want to take it."

"I knew you would."

The doorbell rings with our delivery and we shut down talk of Jean Claude. Neither of us bring up anything but Dexter, food, and Game of Thrones. I let Jean Claude wait until morning. She lets murder wait until morning.

And so, we eat Chinese food while Dexter gives us doggy eyes that can't be resisted. We give him chicken. He farts his appreciation and we end up on the balcony in the cold, hiding from a farting serial killer dog. It's pretty fucking perfect. Except for my secrets. Except for interviews with the police and the uncertainty of the investigation. Those things hang in the air like a fine mist laced with poison.

When we finally head to bed and lay under the covers in the darkness, Abbie whispers, "I don't want anyone to take us from us."

I stroke her hair. "The only ones that can take us from us is one of us, and we aren't going to be foolish enough to allow that to happen."

"I like that answer," she says, relaxing into my side, fingers flexing on my chest. She is tiny and yet she is a force of nature.

She doesn't speak again and I lay there for a good hour after she falls asleep, listening to her breathe, playing all the ways my confessions might go in my head. The one thing I go back to is the delivery. I can't change what happened with Kendall. I don't want to change what happened with Kendall, but I can change how my father affects Abbie. I can make sure that she doesn't feel any more distress by way of my father's manipulation. I slip out of the bed and I whisper for Dexter to stay at the foot of the bed. He's a damn good dog who seems to understand just about anything I tell him. His previous owner must have passed away and then some asshole relative dumped him. Nothing else makes sense. He was loved. I can tell he was loved, and then the anger issues came from losing that love. I relate. That dog is my animal soulmate.

It's midnight when I stand at the window in the living room in pajama bottoms and dial Blake. "If it was a wig," I say without preamble, "it came on and off at some point. What about cameras catching that moment?"

"We tried. We don't have that wig or the coat that was being worn going in and out of the building. Nor does that person show up anywhere on a camera we can hack within a two-mile radius."

"Are there cameras you can't hack?"

"Correction. *Any* camera within a two-mile radius. We hit them all."

"Search my father's house. Get inside. Do what you have to do and take him down if that's what has to happen and if you can't make that happen, I will."

"We don't know that your father did this."

"He did a hell of a lot of other things, so ask me if I care, Blake. He needs to go down."

"You know I don't frame people, Gabe. That's not how we operate."

"I'll fucking frame him if you won't."

"Are you sure you and Reid aren't twins? Because I just had this conversation with him. Both of you are operating emotionally, which isn't your way. Exactly why you both need to step back and give me some room to work. A little birdy tells me there's something in the wind."

"What something?"

"A way out of this. Go to bed and let me do my fucking job. More tomorrow." He hangs up. Fucking asshole hangs up when I'm the one paying him. I shove my phone into my pocket and press my hands to the window. "Damn it," I growl. "Damn his little birdie."

"Gabe?"

I turn as Abbie draws near, wearing only my T-shirt and I notice every part of her, from her wild red mass of curls to her pink painted toes. And her companion: Dexter. He's by her side, her private escort. I drag her to me and settle her against the window. "Miss me?"

"I heard, Gabe. I heard what you just said. I heard you talk about framing your father to save me."

I inhale and look skyward before I level her in a stare, knowing everything I want to protect her from is charging at me, at her, at us. "My father is a bad man, Abbie."

"You keep telling me that, but—"

"He may well be the one who did this, all of it."

She pales. "What?"

"He took over your ex's role in the development project when Kenneth died. He has the most to benefit from his death. Jean Claude—"

"You can't trust Jean Claude. He'd turn this on your father as easily as he'd turn it on us. He did this."

"No. Reid doesn't believe he did it and he knows the man, and yes, well. My brother was involved with him through our father, and for far too long. Furthermore, he's pissed about the police attention. If he did this, it would have looked like an accident."

"Okay," she accepts. "Why would your father do this when he'd benefit, when he'd become a suspect?"

"Because you were a more likely suspect. Why the hell do you think the killer wore a red wig?"

"This doesn't feel right, Gabe. It's not him. This is murder we're talking about."

"You don't know my father. I didn't want you to truly know what he's capable of, but he has killed to get what he wants. He will kill to get what he wants." I release her and walk several steps away before turning to face her. "Kenneth had a bank account in your name. Blake got rid of all records of that account."

"I know nothing about this."

"Of course, you don't. You were never meant to know. My father helped Kenneth launder money through it."

"I—I don't even know what to say to that."

"Say you get it. Say you understand that my father has to be dealt with."

"I mean, yes. I get that Gabe."

"Good. Step one: we need to be done with Jean Claude so he doesn't turn on us. We'll sign the papers right away. I want you off his radar."

"Before what?"

"I didn't say before."

"*Before what?*" she presses.

"Before I end this."

"How?" she asks. "How are you going to end this?"

"I'll turn his crap around on him."

"Are you talking about framing your father?"

"I don't have to frame him. I just have to do what you did to your ex. I just have to give Jean Claude proof that my father crossed him. And then he's over."

"He'll kill him."

"Or ruin him," I say. "Whatever the case, it's what my father deserves."

She walks toward me, stops in front of me. "He's your father."

"Who do you think thought of using a red wig, Abbie? I guarantee you, it was him. He hates me. He wanted to hurt me. I'm why you're in hell right now. My father killed your ex to punish you, therefore, punish me. That's the shitty father I was born to. That's what runs in my blood."

"You don't know that he did this and you aren't like him!"

Suddenly, I'm done wondering if she will run and leave. It's time she takes off the damn rose-colored glasses. It's time we both take this bullet. "You don't think I'm like him? Let's talk about KM. Let's talk about Kendall."

LISA RENEE JONES

CHAPTER THIRTY-SEVEN

gabe

"No," Abbie orders, poking my chest. "No. *Do not* tell me your deep, dark secret as a way to push me away. If you already regret asking me to live with you, you have a get out of jail free pass. I'll leave."

"That's not what this is. I want you here with me. Why the fuck do you think I want to make my father go away?"

"Go away? I don't want to know what that means. And you don't get to use me to justify making him *go away*."

"Use you? That's what you think I'm doing? Using you?"

"What I think, is that you need to go have another drink, Gabe, and get out of your own head."

"You *wanted* to know about KM."

"I wanted to know what affects you, yes. I will always want to know what affects you, but not like this. Not when you're out for blood. You know what you want to do is wrong. That's why you're doing this. You want to become a monster in my mind like you are in yours. Then you can do bad, get rid of me, and wallow in your own hatred for yourself. In other words, you can go back to what you were doing before you met me." Her eyes narrow on me. "You know what? I'm not going to let that happen."

She steps around me and starts walking toward the bedroom. The very act of her putting distance between us cuts me with a knife of emotions that bleed and scream in every part of me. I don't stop her, though. Instead, I turn and watch her walk away. "How is this you not letting this happen? You're leaving?"

"No." She twists around to look at me. "I'm going to bed. *Our* bed. Until you have the balls to tell me that you regret asking me to stay." She doesn't wait for a reply. She starts walking again and damn Dexter goes with her.

She's staying.

For now.

She still doesn't know about KM. That was the entire point of getting past this with her. Knowing she knows. Knowing she'll stay here with me. I should never have asked her to move in with me before I told her. I was selfish. I was an asshole. The demons of the past are clawing at me, biting me. Eating me alive. I want to go after her and force her to listen, but that's all her ex ever did to her: force her to do things his way. I want everything that could tear us apart gone, deleted, but I can't just delete KM.

I scrub my jaw and turn to the window, but where it would normally bring me peace, it just explodes like empty space in my mind. This view is nothing. It's not peace. It's not calm. Abbie is my peace. She's my only path to any version of happiness and damn it to hell, I came home to tell her about Kendall tonight, and not because I wanted to justify attacking my father. Not because I wanted Abbie to leave. Because I was afraid my father would take her from me. Because I wasn't going to let that happen.

Because I'm *not* going to let that happen.

I'm walking before I even register the decision, pursuing Abbie, and yes, Dexter. They are my family now. Or I hope like hell they are. Dexter is the only real sure thing. He won't give a shit what happened with Kendall, but this is a triangle. We're supposed to be a fucking triangle. I want a triangle. I step into the bedroom to find Abbie and Dexter on the bed, side by side. Abbie laying down, the blankets pulled to her chest.

I close the space between me and the bed, and sit down, giving Abbie and Dexter my back. "Kendall was my fiancée," I say.

Abbie jerks to a sitting position behind me and I move to sit next to her. "Don't do this now," Abbie orders. "Don't do this when—"

"Abbie," I say softly, drawing her hand into mine. "It's not as simple as you think. I need to tell you about KM tonight."

"Yesterday you weren't ready to talk about this, Gabe. Now, the minute you invite me into your world, it's like this is a way to push me away again. I don't like it. You're messing with my emotions. You're messing with us, our future. Whatever that is."

"Our future is up to you. I know what I want and that's you, here."

"I don't know if I believe you."

It's then that I'm reminded that Abbie has trust issues, just like I do. That Abbie and I have more in common than I choose to remember, because I have my past buried, or I did, until I met her. Until the past has to be faced for us to move forward.

"You weren't ready to talk about this, Gabe," she repeats, her voice a raspy whisper. "You weren't ready. I said I'd give you space and time. That was hard to do, but I did it. Now, this."

"And it meant the world to me that you blindly trusted me because I know your ex made trust a challenge. I know this for reasons that run deep and personal. As for being ready to tell you, I will never be ready to tell you anything that I think might make you walk away, Abbie. Never."

"Yet you want to tell me now? I'm *very* damn confused, Gabe."

"Telling you about my past isn't about pushing you away. It's the opposite. I'm going to go after my father because he hurts people. Because he will hurt you if I give him the chance. When I do, he'll come at us. He'll tell you about KM because he knows. He's the only one who knows. I need to tell you before he tells you."

Understanding seeps into her eyes and she throws away the blanket and settles her feet on the floor, scooting closer to me, taking my hand. "Tell me," she urges softly, "but whatever this is, it's not the bullet you think it is. I promise you."

"I'm not a gentle man."

"Dexter and I disagree."

Her and Dexter. My heart swells with happiness and regret, with fear. So damn much fear that I will love them and lose them. And yet, I have to press her to see all that I am before someone else does. "You do remember that I told a bookie where to find my sister's stalker and he ended up in the hospital, right?"

"You were protecting her. I get that."

"You didn't even ask me if I talked to the police," I point out.

"I know you did."

"How, Abbie?"

"Because *I know*. Did you?"

"Yes. Reid and I did, Reese did. Cat did. But the police had limitations, too many limitations." I study her, search for doubt, but there is none. That's going to change. I turn away from her and I could hesitate, but I don't. I've made the decision to tell her this story. I'm not going to choke on it. "Kendall and I met while working at the same law firm."

"For your father?"

"No. I wanted to find my own way. I interned and planned to work at another firm. We were both up and coming, focused on our careers, with a plan for marriage and family. I loved her, Abbie. Or I thought I did. I believed I did." I cut my stare and inhale, drawing in a hard-earned breath. "And then—" I let the words trail off and I must revel in the silence too long because Abbie prods me.

"And then?"

"And then, suddenly, she was pregnant. It wasn't our plan but I was happy. I wanted a family. I wanted the two kids and two dogs and a damn cat. I embraced the fuck out of it. I took care of her while she threw up. I was there for the first sonogram. I was there for every fucking thing until I wasn't." My voice radiates with anger I didn't know I still felt, but talking about this cuts me, fresh blood seeping into the story of my life.

"What happened?" she prods.

And then what—

This is where the real story begins.

LISA RENEE JONES

CHAPTER THIRTY-EIGHT

gabe

I don't hesitate to continue. I've committed. I'm telling this story my way before my father tells it his way.

"The baby wasn't mine. It was my best friend, Mike's baby."

The blood drains from Abbie's face. She swallows hard. "How did you find out?"

"Mike worked with us at my father's firm. They were working late and they thought that I'd left for a meeting. I hadn't. I went looking for Kendall to tell her it was cancelled and to take her to dinner. Instead, I overheard them talking. Mike had apparently made some bad financial decisions while she'd managed to forget to take a few pills and get pregnant. They knew it wasn't mine, because it was timed during a trip I'd taken with a client out of the country. A *two-month-long* trip to Japan. I listened as they decided that she'd go through with marrying me, even convince me to elope. Then she'd take a chunk of my money in a dirty divorce. They'd then raise the kid on my money."

"Oh God. This all makes sense now. That's why you—that's why—"

"Yes. That's why I got snipped. So no other woman could use my damn babymakers as a weapon against me."

"I would never—"

"I know that, Abbie, but I didn't plan on meeting you. I didn't plan on wanting a woman beyond a fast fuck ever again." I don't give her time to ask questions. I go on. "And I know you know I'm not done yet. You know that's not where the story ends."

"You made her pay," she assumes.

"I did what your ex did to people who crossed him, Abbie."

She stiffens ever so slightly but she doesn't pull away. "What does that mean?"

"I wanted revenge. I'm not proud of that, but I did."

"You hurt them."

"Yes."

"How?" she presses.

"Do the details matter?"

"Yes," she says. "I believe they do or—" Her brows dip. "Where is Kendall now?"

"I don't know and I don't care."

"And the baby?" she asks.

"A teenager in a fancy prep school."

"And Mike?"

"He's dead, Abbie. My ex-best friend is dead." I stand up and turn to face her. Dexter scoots closer to her, nudges her hand to pet him, letting her know that he's there for her. The way I want to be there for her.

"Tell me," she orders softly.

"I wanted revenge. I'm not proud of that but I did. I called the one person I knew would know how to make that happen."

"Your father."

"Yes, and I told him that I wanted Mike ruined. I didn't give him limits."

"Did you know what that meant with your father at the time?" she surprises me by asking.

"No. I didn't know what that meant with my father at the time, but I damn sure do now."

"What did he do?"

"It didn't take much. I had no idea that Mike's family was into some shady shit. My father made sure it went public. They lost everything and Mike killed himself."

She covers her mouth on a gasp. "You didn't do that to him. You didn't—"

"I ordered the ruin of a man and he killed himself, Abbie. Don't even think about softening that blow."

"And Kendall? What did your dad do to her?"

"He didn't. That was all me. I ruined her myself. We'd had some issues over ethics violations she refused to see as an issue. I made sure they were exposed. She was disbarred. She gave birth and put the baby up for adoption."

She stares up at me, seconds ticking by. "Where's the baby now?"

"He's a teenager who was adopted by a good family. Word is that he may well end up in an Ivy League school."

"Which you know because you helped him."

"I know because I'm the one who stole his parents from him."

She stands up and walks toward me, closing the few steps between us. "Because you helped him. Because you look out for him."

"A child will never know his mother or father because of me."

"Stop making yourself into a monster."

"Stop making me into a hero who helped a child that only needed help because of what I did."

"His parents were corrupt, Gabe. And what you did wasn't kind, but you didn't kill anyone. You didn't set Mike's family up and make it look like they did things they didn't do. That's what Kenneth would have done and from what you tell me, that's what your father would have done. And that angers me. You were young. You took guidance from your father. He could have taught you to move on, but he didn't do that."

"I've gone after people, Abbie."

"Have you ever killed anyone?"

"No."

"Have you ever broken the law to hurt someone?"

"No."

"Revenge is dangerous. What you did wasn't kind. It wasn't forgiving but you have to forgive yourself. I do. I forgive you."

I tangle my fingers into her hair and pull her close. "Abbie," I breathe out. "Damn it, you need to really look at me. I don't want you to see one thing now, and then later, when I can't live without you, see something else. See me now. Be angry. Make me fight past that anger so that I know you see all of me."

"I do and thank God for it. One of us has to. You see your father when you look in the mirror. I see you, the *real* you, the man who fights for those he loves. The man who saves animals and babies. A man who would have been an amazing father. And if it's the last thing I do on this earth, you will see you the way I see you."

Her words punch me in the gut. She sees the man I want to be. The man I had a chance to be but that man is long gone. That's a problem for us both. "You have on rose-colored glasses and one day you'll take them off, you will see the real me and that shock will drive you away, the way my mother woke up and warned us not to be like the man she'd once loved."

Her hands come down on my face. "I don't believe that you would do the things your father does. The things my ex-husband did."

"My blood—"

"Is also your mothers and your mind is your own. Your actions are your own. You were young. Would you go to your father for revenge now that you are older, wiser, and you know him as the monster, not the man?"

"Never. I'd go to my mother who Reid and I should have idolized over my fucking father."

"Your mother would be proud of you, Gabe, because you learned that lesson. Because you're not your father. And knowing that you could have been, that one piece of your life could have sent you that direction, not this direction, matters. I have never wanted to be an 'us' more than I do with you and Dexter." She presses her lips to mine and whispers. "You are already my best friend."

I rotate her and lay her down on the bed, shifting to slide my leg between hers, my body angled to hers. "And you, Abbie, are my best friend."

"Best friends don't use rose-colored glasses, Gabe. They see perfection in the imperfect."

Those words, radiate through me and spin ten emotions I don't try to name. Instead, I kiss her because I want to, and because if I don't, I'll confess my love. And it's too soon for love when, despite her denial, she still wears rose-colored glasses. I fear she just doesn't know it yet.

LISA RENEE JONES

CHAPTER THIRTY-NINE

gabe

I lay awake holding Abbie, with Dexter at the foot of the bed, a surreal sense of rightness to the three of us together. Until these two came into my life, rightness meant alone. Rightness meant no one really knew me. No one at all. Not even Reid. Hell, the truth is that I always felt my father knew me better than anyone because of the past, and his role in Kendall and Mike's undoing.

Did I blow my past into more than it had to be? Or did Abbie, downplay my sins because contrary to her vow not to, she's falling in love with her best friend? Holy hell I want her to fall in love with me. I want and want and want some fucking more with this woman.

That thought was the last thought I had when I fell asleep and the first I have in the new day.

Exactly why I wake Abbie by kissing every part of her body I can possibly kiss, her soft sweet moans, the best damn way a man, this man, could wake up. I don't fuck her. I make love to her and when we're done, there's a warmth between us that expands like a fire casting a glow across a cold room. We're the fire that does more than cast me in warmth. We ignite fuel in me to take action. To shut my father down once and for all. To make everything bad in our lives right now good.

Still in a playful mood, Abbie mentions the shower and I proceed to carry her there, depositing her into the hot water, and then thanks to Dexter's demands, leave her there alone. He needs to pee. Damn cute fucking dog. I throw on sweats and a T-shirt to take him out, avoiding the front of the building when the building staff warns me of reporters. A necessity that has me dialing Reid. "We got rid of him but we didn't deal with him."

I don't have to say who "him" is. "Exactly what kept me up all night," he admits. "We should meet."

"Agreed. I need to get Abbie to the office and settled but I don't want to talk there."

"The coffee shop," he says, referencing the spot by the office we often meet. "Ten AM."

"Ten AM." We disconnect and I head back upstairs to feed Dexter.

I enter the bedroom already peeling away my T-shirt and toeing off my shoes. "Your dog licked the doorman from chin to forehead," I call out, walking toward the open bathroom door. "And I'm talking full-on lips-to-tongue action." I find her at one of the two double sinks, a silk robe hugging her curves.

"My dog?" she laughs, turning to face me, a lacy black bra teasing me through the gaping V of the silk robe.

"I've decided he's your dog when he does shit like that," I say, dragging her to me and squeezing her backside. "I could really get used to this view in the morning."

"You better. I'm moving in, remember?"

"I do. When Abbie?"

"You tell me?"

"Now."

"Now?" she laughs.

"Yes. We'll get all we can ourselves this weekend and call movers to get the rest."

"I have a lease."

"I'll pay it."

"You are not—"

I mold her to me and kiss her. "What's mine is yours. We'll work out the details later, but you will never want for anything ever again. You have my word." I kiss her again and walk to the shower, undressing and stepping inside, pulling the door shut.

It opens again and Abbie stands there, tempting me to pull her inside, and if her hair wasn't dry and her make-up done, I would. Hell if I didn't have the meeting with Reid, I'd do it anyway and she could just get dressed all over again.

"I don't want your money. I've had money, remember? It didn't keep me warm at night or make me laugh, or even moan like you do, Gabe. And I don't want to be taken care of. I want to be equal. I want to be friends. I want you, Gabe Maxwell, and nothing more." And with that, she shuts the door and disappears, leaving me with more of that warmth spreading through me, as does my determination to do just what she said I shouldn't.

Take care of her.

Whatever that has to mean. Whoever I have to cross. Even Jean Claude. I don't care how dangerous he is, he's not as dangerous as a man protecting the woman who woke him up.

Abbie and I drink coffee in the kitchen, our kitchen, and talk through the plans to move her out of her place. Dexter is exceptionally excited, feeding off our energy and laughter as we talk about what furniture she wants to keep. "We can redecorate," I offer. "Anything you want."

"Really?" she challenges, sipping from my coffee cup when hers is out of reach, comfortable. We're remarkably comfortable with each other. "Because I was thinking a pink theme. Pink blinds. Pink rugs. I have a thing for pink."

"Then we'll decorate in fucking pink rugs and blinds, baby."

"Good," she says. "I can't wait to go shopping."

We laugh together, give Dexter goodbye affection and a bone before we decide to make the short walk to the office. "Talk to your mother about the shelter," I say. "If she can't get a place secured, find some options. Let's start looking."

"You're sure about this, Gabe?"

"Tax write-off, baby. Is there another shelter we could buyout and merge with? A shelter we could improve? Turn it into a doggy spa shelter?"

"A doggy spa," she laughs. "I like that idea. And maybe. I'll talk to my mother."

We chat that out a bit more, including the merits of doggy manicures, and we've just walked into the office to be greeted by Lulu who is apparently back from Italy today. I should know this of course, she is my assistant, but hell if I did. I introduce her to Abbie and since she's also a redhead, the comparison is awkward. The looks Lulu casts between me and Abbie are as well. She knows me. She senses something between us, but I'll have to have the "zip your lips" conversation with her.

When I'm finally in Abbie's office with her alone, she arches a brow. "You don't like redheads?"

"I don't care what color her hair is when she kicks everyone's ass for me, and she does, you'll like her."

"I do, but I think she knows about us."

"She knows me," I say, repeating my earlier thoughts out loud. "She reads me. She, no doubt, knows about us because of those things but she'll zip her lips. She's good like that."

"I didn't even think about how living together might make us more obviously a couple here at work. We live right around the corner. We could be seen in the area walking around arm in arm."

We live.

HER SUBMISSION

I fucking love how easily she merges our worlds. "I don't think we should hide our relationship," I say sitting on the corner of her desk as she claims her chair. "As we discussed, you're it, baby. You're the one launching our much-needed charity division for the company. If someone tries to throw stones at you, they're going to look like shit. Besides, Reid and his wife work together. But we'll handle us how you want to handle us with the staff."

My cellphone rings and I snag it from my pocket and glance at the Caller ID. "Reese," I say, answering on speaker. "You have me and Abbie on the line."

"Just what I hoped for," he says. "Listen, I'm going into court, but I got some news. Blake got off-the-record word on an arrest being made today. A man named Neal, who was doing some work for Kenneth. Apparently, Kenneth was cutting him out of the new complex which meant cutting him out of big money. Neal killed him before he could make the cut."

"I knew Neal," Abbie says, sitting up straighter. "He did dirty work for Kenneth. I know he did. I overhead conversations."

"And Neal knows you," Reese replies. "Law enforcement believes that he used a wig to make the murder look like you did it but the crime scene was too professional for that to fly. I have to go, but hang tight for more news. Once the arrest is made, Blake or myself will update you both."

"Will we still be interviewed?" Abbie asks quickly.

"I'll know more soon," Reese says. "I suspect we'll know a lot of things today."

He says a hasty goodbye and then disconnects. My phone immediately buzzes with a text and I glance down to find a message from Reid: *Two plus two does not equal four. I'm headed to the coffee shop now.*

My jaw tenses at an old saying my father used to use when telling us to look beyond the obvious. In other words, my father's involved.

"Gabe? Something wrong?"

I shove my phone back in my pocket. "Reid is waiting on me to talk about the agreement with Jean Claude. And as for what's wrong? It sounds like a lot of right, baby."

"Could this really be over?" Abbie asks hopefully.

I stand and pull her to her feet. "It will be soon," I say, stroking her cheek. "And then you'll be free to fall in love with me."

"I told you. I will not fall in love with you, Gabe."

"And I will not fall in love with you, Abbie."

We smile and it's a united smile, one that says we both know this is a game. One we both win. "Call your mom. Make sure she knows what's going on. Find us a shelter location. Let's save some animals while we're not falling in love."

"I like that idea."

"Good. I need to take care of Jean Claude, among other things. I'll be back soon." I kiss her hand and head to the door, with the intent of meeting up with Reid. Kenneth's murder might be solved, but another problem is not. My father.

"Gabe," Abbie says, as I'm about to open the door.

I pause, and I know without looking at her that she read me, when I thought she hadn't. I glance over my shoulder. "Yes?"

"You aren't your father. Don't forget that."

My jaw clenches. Yes. She knows. She damn sure knows that I'm after blood and my father. "No," I say, agreeing with her. "I'm not like my father." And with that, I leave. She's right. I'm not my father. I don't hurt people for personal gain. I don't turn my back on those I care about and I'm not going to start now.

Abbie's the reason this is over for my father.

She's the reason he won't be able to hurt anyone else.

She's the best thing that ever happened to me and anyone who has ever known my father.

LISA RENEE JONES

CHAPTER FORTY

gabe

I'm barely out of Abbie's office when Lulu steps in front of me. "You had an interesting time while I was gone, I see."

"Not now. I need to go."

"I'll walk with you," she says, as she often does. "I have a few messages for you."

"Save them. Get rid of them. No time for them. But yes. Walk with me."

She nods, and we fall into step, but we don't speak until we're on the elevator alone. "Yes, I'm seeing Abbie. We're moving in together. No, I don't want anyone to know until she wants them to know. That's Abbie's call."

"You don't like staying silent about it," she observes. "She'll come out of the closet when she trusts you. Not until."

I feel that assessment as accurate and painful. She wants to trust me. Some part of her does trust me, but her ex was horrible to her. He burned her. Time builds trust. We need time that's about our life as normal human beings, not murder suspects. "You know about—"

"The murder? Yes. I know. What can I do?"

I update her on the arrest. "That's good news," she says. "And again. What can I do?"

"What you always do. Control the sharks biting at my feet. And protect Abbie."

Her eyes soften. "I will. Like she was my very own boss and friend."

She's telling me I'm a friend. "Friend," I say softly, because we both know I don't have many. I don't let people close to me.

The elevator opens and I leave her in the car, thankful she's back and a friend who will be Abbie's friend, too. I'm comforted by this thought and walk through the lobby with a focus I might not have without her presence watching over Abbie. It's a short walk and not long before I'm sitting in a corner booth with my brother.

"Neal, the guy they're arresting today," Reid says, "he did work for dad. A lot of work. He'll know I know. He'll know that he has to be behind that red wig." He jabs the table. "He came at my wife. Now he came at your woman. I'm so fucking done with him."

In this moment, I realize how lucky I am to have Reid and Cat. They aren't like my father. Reid, who came the closest to that demise, still didn't become that monster. "We need to be done with him," I say. "We tried and failed. We can't fail again."

"I have dirt on him," Reid says. "The problem is he has dirt on me, too."

"His dirt he linked to you to control you."

"If you go at him," Reid says, "he'll come at me."

"And you'll take him down with you. He knows that."

"But I'll go down and that hurts my wife." He scrubs his jaw. "And man, no one knows yet, but Carrie's talking about babies more and more often as Cat gets closer to her due date."

Babies.

This announcement thunders through me. Both of my siblings with babies, while I made sure I can't be a father. Abbie's affected by my decision. I shove that aside and focus on the here and now. "Then let's talk about how we end this before any more Maxwells are running around. What if we get him to confess while we record him? Then turn him in."

"He'll lash out and come at us, even behind bars. You know that."

"Aside from killing him, Reid, which would make mom roll over in her grave, what else?"

"I don't disagree with sending him to jail. It just can't seem like we're involved."

"What do you suggest?"

"Let's go meet with Walker Security. Blake can make this happen. He has the connections and the hacking skills to set him up."

"Blake's going to agree to this?"

"If it's a real crime, yes. I believe he will, but you know this will be bad press for the company. He's the founder. He's our father."

"I don't care about bad press. We have a solid foundation. We can handle it. Our family, our women, that's what matters. We can't keep swimming in the same shark-infested waters and expect to survive. We have to get rid of the shark. Let's go meet with Blake."

I've just hung up with the dog walker when my mother returns my call. "You heard they made an arrest for Kenneth's murder?" I ask.

"I heard. Thank God. It sounds like this is over."

Over.

Why do I feel like that's not true?

"How do you feel about it, Abigail?" my mother asks. "*Is it* over?"

"I hope so. Reese says we'll know more later today."

"I'm eager for news. You know, I was thinking earlier. Gabe's really taken care of us, honey."

"I know. He has. He's—well, I'm moving in with him."

"Wow. Well, I'd say that's fast, but, drumroll please, I'm moving in with Brandon, too."

My eyes go wide. "What? You are?" I'm a bit stunned. My mother has always been all work, no love life. "When?"

"Soon. Now. I might as well already live with him here in the Hamptons. I'm always with him. And since Gabe has a place here we can still see each other often."

"Wait. The Hamptons? He doesn't have a place here?"

"No, Abigail. We'll live here."

"You can't keep the shelter in the Hamptons, mom," I say. "How is that going to work?"

"Brandon's going to let me keep it here at the ranch and Reid already talked to me about the offer on the shelter there in the city. He's scanning me the paperwork to sign. You're a go on that, right?"

"Yes, I think that's the right decision. We need to let Jean Claude forget who we are but that doesn't mean we can't find another location here. I mean how many people are there in the Hamptons to adopt the animals? Isn't that limiting for the animals?"

"He has ideas on how to overcome that, and with all the money here, the donations and support will be overflowing."

We talk through the details and she actually seems to be happy and has a really amazing plan. "I feel a little lost," I say. "I'm used to helping you with the shelter."

"You still can, but now you can do other things as well. When can you come up here?"

"We're moving me this weekend so probably not until the weekend after next."

"Do you want help moving?"

"Maybe. If you can?"

"Of course. Me and Brandon will come." She hesitates. "Abigail, honey, the memorial or funeral, or whatever it is they're holding for Kenneth, is set for Monday. I'm not sure why it's so far out, but what's your plan?"

I know that Reese says I don't have to go, but there is a part of me that feels bad for Kenneth. He has no living family but I certainly wasn't his family, either. "You were divorced, Abbie," my mother says softly. "Let's skip it."

I don't need a lot of persuading. "I do feel weird about going to the funeral of a man I despised. It feels wrong."

"Agreed. Decision made. We aren't going."

I let her guide me on this. We aren't going to the funeral.

We've just finished our chat and disconnected when a strange number appears on my phone. I frown, wondering if it's Reese calling from the courthouse or even the police trying to reach me. Nervously, I hit the answer button. "This is Abbie."

"Abbie. This is Gabe's father."

Shock radiates through me and then fear for Gabe. "I—how did you get this number?"

"The dog walker gave it to me when I tipped her and told her I'd finish walking Dexter. He's here with me, at my apartment. Come pick him up and we can have a nice chat."

"I'll send Gabe to get him."

"That won't work for me or you. There are some things about my son you need to know that he won't allow me to share if he comes along. And hurry. I really don't like dogs. I'd hate to just let Dexter run loose in the city. There are a great deal of cars here, now aren't there?"

LISA RENEE JONES

CHAPTER FORTY-ONE

abbie

Dexter has been kidnapped.

It's like my child has been kidnapped.

I love that dog and so does Gabe. We love that boy. He trusts us. He won't understand what's happening. Maybe he'll think he's being taken back to a shelter. I tunnel my fingers through my hair and try to think about what to do. Don't call Gabe, his father had said. Or he'll send Dexter into moving traffic. What kind of person even says something like that?

I push to my feet and start to pace. I want to call Gabe, but he's itching for an excuse to lash out at his father. Obviously, he has good reason, but I'm not going to lose that man to a jail cell. I'm not stupid enough to go to his father, either. Gabe isn't an exaggerator about his father, clearly. I could call Reid, but he and Gabe together might be the worst possible thing to happen.

Dexter was named Dexter for a reason, I remind myself. Gabe has seen him show a mean side. He'll be fine. He'll take care of himself until I get to him. Only I've never seen any mean side of Dexter, and when a dog acts out, often the receiver of the dog's anger acts out as well. Worry fills me. I have to make a decision here. Call Gabe? Call Reid? Call Cat, maybe? She knows her brothers as well as her father, but she's pregnant. Gabe worries about her.

There's a knock on the door and Lulu sticks her head in. "Can I—"

"Come in," I say, motioning her forward, aware after this morning that she is well-trusted by Gabe. "Shut the door."

Looking alarmed, she steps inside the office and shuts the door. "What's wrong?"

"Gabe's father. How bad is he?"

"A monster," she says quickly. "I hate that man and I swear at times I've believed he wasn't even Gabe's true father. There's no way his blood is of his blood. Why?" She doesn't give me time to answer, but my face must tell a story. "Oh God. Gabe loves you so his father is attacking you."

Gabe loves me.

We've teased about this idea but hearing someone else say it— "Did he tell you he loves me?"

"He doesn't have to tell me, silly girl. I know him. I see the way he looks at you. I feel it when he talks about you."

Gabe loves me.

I love Gabe.

It's too soon for such things and yet—this man is my life.

"What did he do to you?" she presses.

"How easily do you believe Gabe would go after his father at all costs?"

"Far easier than he'd admit. Why? *What* is happening?"

"His father kidnapped our dog to get me to come to him, to use me and Dexter against Gabe. I need to make a fast decision now. So here are the options I think I have before me—"

Reid and I end up at Walker Security looking for outside resources that protect our families, and the company's reputation. We're trying to deal with our father objectively and smartly. But deal we must, of this we both agree. We sit in a conference room side by side, across from Blake and his man, Savage, talking through options to leash our father once and for all.

"Sometimes," I say, "I feel like we're caught in a superhero movie, the same villain to fight over and over. I used to be Batman and now, I'm Superman thanks to my own Lois Lane. I can't kill the bastard."

"Amen to that," Blake and Reid both say.

"Been there," Blake says.

"Living that," Reid adds.

"I'm not," Savage interjects. "I'm fucking Batman on steroids. You want him dead?"

I'd laugh, but this is Savage, a former Green Beret, with a long scar down his cheek, and a crazy fucking attitude. He could well be serious. "It would be easier."

"The world would be a better place," Reid agrees, and we both share a look. We're not serious about killing him, but we both believe he's pure evil.

"Let's talk about Superman options," Blake says, the reason in the room.

"Jail time or shipping him off to another country," I suggest.

"Another country is a better option," Reid replies, "at least from our company perspective, but how do we do that and ensure he's gone? Really gone? He can't cause trouble."

"The only thing he understands is threats," I say.

"And our threats have proven less than effective," Reid reminds me. "He keeps fucking showing up, like acid in a rainstorm."

"Then you haven't used the right ammunition," Blake replies.

"And he feels no fear," Savage adds. "Fear motivates men, even those who like to seem as if they feel no fear."

"How do you motivate fear in those who have a high ceiling?" I ask. "That's the real question."

"Money," Reid says. "He doesn't want to be without it."

"That's not enough," I say, throwing out another idea. "Prison. Real fear of prison."

"We tried that once," Reid counters. "We have the ammunition to put him in jail. I have proof of many of his crimes."

"He linked you to his crimes to control us," I remind him.

"Then it can't come from us," he says.

"Jean Claude," I supply.

"We don't want to owe Jean Claude," Reid says. "That's holding us prisoner as well. He'd go after our women."

Blake's phone rings and he glances down at the number and frowns before hitting the answer button. "Abbie?"

I stiffen, sharing a look with Reid before watching Blake's face. "When?" he asks. "No. You did absolutely right by calling me. Don't do anything. I've got this handled. More soon." He disconnects.

"What the fuck?" I demand. "What's handled?"

"You. She called me because she was afraid you'd go after your father."

"I told her I was going after him. Damn it." I scrub my jaw. "What is she thinking?"

"That your father went after you this morning."

My eyes narrow and ice slides down my spine. "What does that mean?"

"Yes," Reid states. "What does that mean?"

"Your father kidnapped Dexter from the dog walker and then called Abbie and told her to come get Dexter. He told her that if she told you, he'd let Dexter run free in traffic."

I curse and stand up. "That's fucking priceless. Fuck Superman. I'm going to kill him." I turn to the door and Savage steps in front of me.

"Think first," Savage says while Reid joins me.

"Move, Savage," Reid orders.

"Both of you deep breathe and talk to me," Blake interjects.

Reid and I whirl on him. "We need to deal with this," I say. "Now, before my damn dog gets hurt."

"Abbie called me for a reason, Gabe," Blake replies, on his feet now. "She doesn't want you to end up in jail. What's your father's endgame?"

Reid looks at me. "He doesn't know we made the agreement with Jean Claude. He's trying to get it signed."

"And he wants his money from the real estate development deal." My lips thin. "The same reason he had Abbie's ex-husband killed. Damn it, I need to get to Dexter."

"We'll go together," Blake says. "You and me. Just you and me." He pats the gun at his hip. "And my weapon. If anyone takes action, it's me and if you press that, I'll hit you with the damn thing."

"I'm coming," Reid replies. "You need me. He'll use me against Gabe and he can't do that when I'm there."

"Well, fuck," Blake murmurs. "I guess we're all going."

I eye Savage. "Get Abbie. Take her home so when I get there with Dexter she'll be able to see him."

"What do you want me to tell her?"

"That she's right. I'm not my father."

With that, Reid and I exchange a look of understanding. We might want to hurt that bastard, but all the women in our lives, including our mother, want him saved. So we'll save him. Unless he hurts my damn dog. Then he dies.

LISA RENEE JONES

CHAPTER FORTY-TWO

gabe

Abbie and Dexter are my world now. My father is pushing my buttons, buttons that he's foolish to push, but I also know that he's a master of manipulation. He wants me flustered. He wants to find those hotspots I control and he now wants to control.

Exactly why I don't call Abbie on the way to my father's apartment. It's a short drive and I can't afford to hear her fear-laden voice, not if I don't want to do something I'll regret.

"Do I need to point out that we have no plan?" Reid asks, sitting next to me while Blake rides up front with one of his men behind the wheel.

"Get my fucking dog back," I say. "And tell him he's too fucking late on the property deal for the shelter. You already made it with Jean Claude."

"The bigger picture," Reid reminds me. "We aren't dealing with the bigger picture."

"We'll deal with it when my dog isn't in danger."

The SUV stops in front of my father's building and I'm out before Blake or Reid can object. I'm at the building door by the time they appear on either side of me.

"We need to stop and talk," Blake says. "We need a plan."

"I've stated the plan already," I reply, opening the door and entering the lobby. "Taking Dexter home." I walk to the security desk.

"Mr. Maxwell," the guard, a tall, lanky man in his fifties, greets. "Go on up. He said to expect you."

"Of course he did," I murmur while the guard nods to Reid. "Welcome, sir."

I start walking and Reid and Blake are quick to join me. Neither of them speak. They get the point. I'm here for one reason: my dog. Anger radiates through me, but I'm calm because calm is the best way to get Dexter back and to protect my woman and my dog. It's a practiced calm, the kind Kendall taught me. Rage and fury get you nowhere. Calculation does. I punch the elevator button and the doors open. The three of us step inside and ride in silence to my father's floor, where we exit, also in silence, an air of readiness between us. I wouldn't want to be my father right now, and yet, this is what he wanted.

He wanted me.

He wanted Reid.

He also gets Blake.

This was never about Abbie. This was about the two sons who pushed him out of the business he started before he destroyed us and it, and everyone involved. He's a criminal. It's time to stop walking around that. It's time to stop walking a ledge with him. One way or the other, this ends and if it's not today, it's tomorrow. I'm done with him. Abbie is done with him and will never even meet him. We're almost at the door of our destination when it opens.

To my shock, a familiar man with regal features, in an expensive suit exits the room with Dexter by his side. Dexter starts to bark and launches himself forward, toward me, happy as can be. I squat to greet him, and Jean Claude releases the leash, allowing Dexter to return to me. What mind fuckery is this?

HER SUBMISSION

"Jean Claude," Reid greets him while Dexter licks my face. I give him a quick ear scratch and stand up.

"Jean Claude," I greet as well, and while I don't know the man well, I do know he still has a throat. In other words, Dexter is a failed serial killer. We need to work on that and soon. "You're not the person I expected to find kidnapping my dog."

"I'm not the person you expected to save your dog," Jean Claude counters.

"Why would you save my dog?" I ask.

"Because I'm exhausted by your father's games that end up on my playground." He gets right to the point. "Neal was hired by him to kill Kenneth. A stupid mistake that brought me unwanted attention. Neal is graciously taking the blow for all of us. He will not name names. I'm sparing your father for the time being because killing him would only bring me more attention, but I don't promise to spare him forever. For now, I've told your father he needs to leave and leave now. If he's smart, he'll make sure he's not easy to find."

"We don't give a fuck what happens to him," Reid replies, pushing back and with a reason he makes clear. "This isn't a favor for me or us. We don't owe you a debt."

"I owe you," Jean Claude counters. "Not only do you protect me loyally even today, after parting ways years before, you made the property deal happen. I called Abbie an hour ago." He looks at me. "As did you. I traded Abbie a signature for the dog, though she assured me she'd sign anyway. I believed her." He looks between us. "He tells me he might go to Europe. Make sure he does." He steps around us and stops next to Blake. "Hack for me."

"Never fucking happening," Blake replies.

Jean Claude laughs. "I had a feeling that'd be your answer." He says nothing more. He simply steps around me and leaves.

I kneel to pet Dexter again and Reid and I share a look. "Do you want to talk to dad?" Reid asks.

"Not if we want him to live," I say, standing up again. "Tell him goodbye and fuck you for me. I'm taking my dog home."

"I'll stay with Reid," Blake says and looks between us. "And I'll make sure your father is supervised until he leaves the country. Seems like this is just what you both wanted."

No, I think. We wanted a father who was a good man, the kind ours can never become. And we wish that we'd figured that out when our mother was alive. All the more reason to cherish the people we have in our lives.

It's twenty minutes later when Dexter and I arrive home and the minute I open the door, Abbie is running toward us. We launch ourselves in her direction and she all but slams into me, immediately trying to explain herself. "I wanted to tell you, but—"

I kiss her. "I know why you told Blake. It was a smart decision. I might have killed him and then you'd have to visit me in jail and that would get complicated."

Dexter barks and Abbie laughs, tears streaming down her face as she kneels and ends up tackled. Savage silently walks past her, giving me a nod and exiting the apartment. I lock the door and go down on the floor next to Abbie. It's a long time later when Dexter calms down and the doggy attacks are over. Abbie and I don't get up. We lay there and stare at each other.

"I was afraid we'd lose him," she whispers, her fingers curling on my jaw as we both roll to our sides and face each other.

"Never," I promise. "You're never going to lose him or me, Abbie."

"Just so you know, Gabe, I don't think I can help but fall in love with you. If that's a problem then—"

I cup her head and kiss her, a deep stroke of tongue before I whisper, "I've loved you since you kissed me by the bathroom in that bar. I love you, Abbie."

"I love you, too, Gabe."

Dexter barks his love and we both laugh. "He loves us, too," I say, before I stand, scoop Abbie up and carry her toward the bedroom where I intend to show her how much I love every inch of her, tonight and as many nights as she allows me. All of the nights she will ever live. Because she's the reason I live.

LISA RENEE JONES

CHAPTER FORTY-THREE

reid

I enter my father's apartment to find him sitting in one of two chairs that faces a window overlooking the city. I sit down next to him. I don't speak. Seconds stretch to minutes before he says, "There's a small town in Italy I'm quite fond of. I'll leave tomorrow morning."

I feel those words in an explosion of emotions. He's my father. He's a bastard. He's leaving. I'll probably never see him again because we both know he's not going where he says he's going. We both know he can't afford to have Jean Claude find him.

"I'll give you a ride to the airport right after you pay off that woman trying to extort us on your behalf."

"You pay her the fuck off and I'll give myself a ride to the airport." He looks over at me. "I'll be back when the baby is born." His expression is defiant. There's no love for Cat and his future grandbaby. It's his way of telling me that I can't get rid of him, not until he's in his grave.

My father underestimates Jean Claude.

Or perhaps Gabe and I underestimate our father, and he'll be back here causing trouble, proving Gabe's superhero-villain-that-won't-die theory. Whatever the case, I walk to the front desk, open the drawer, pull out the checkbook I knew would be there, and point. "Write a check to the woman. Or should I ask Jean Claude to pay your debt?"

He smirks, amused, like he's proud of me for outsmarting him. I really fucking hate when he makes me feel like a chip off the old block but he writes the check and hands it to me. I happily take it. "Happy now?"

"Like a pig rolling in your shit," I say and I am because at least for now, maybe forever, he's leaving, and we'll have peace. I don't say another word. I walk to the door with one intention: going home to my wife and holding her closely, because my father has a way of making me appreciate how damn lucky I am to have her. At least for now, this is over and my brother has finally found his way, outside any path my father influenced. If we're lucky, we'll have Cat's baby and another Maxwell wedding in the near future.

CHAPTER FORTY-FOUR

abbie

Packing up my apartment on Saturday is surreal in all kinds of ways, as is the funeral for Kenneth that has come and gone now without my presence. A chapter or even ten, of my life, it seems, have closed. For Gabe, too, where his father's concerned. He and Reid had confirmed the claim this morning by stopping by his apartment to find him gone. Blake confirmed he found a flight out of the country for him as well.

"Any regrets?" Gabe asks as a group of movers leaves with the last of my furniture, which I've donated to a charity.

"None," I say. "None at all."

He smiles and kisses me. "Then let's go home."

Hours later, I'm in his office that we're sharing now, filing away some of my basic documents, like my birth certificate, when I find a bag with a couple of cellphones in it. Gabe appears in the doorway, looking sexy as hell in a simple white tee and jeans. This man is mine. I am his. Does life get any better?

"You want a glass of wine?"

Apparently, it does. With wine. "I'd love a glass." I hold up the bag of cellphones. "Do you secretly run a cellphone store and I don't know it?"

His jaw clenches and looks skyward before he closes the space between us and kneels in front of me. "Rose-colored glasses, Abbie? Is that how you really want to see me and us?"

I inhale and let it out, and I don't know why, but I know what this is. "You used them when you were planning to ruin Kenneth." Surprise flickers in his eyes. "I told you. I don't see you with rose-colored glasses. And you told me you tried to ruin him. Am I right about the phones?"

"Yes," he confirms. "I hired someone I knew had shit for morals, and told him to dig. Kenneth died before he even got back to me. That's the honest to God truth."

He expects me to one day wake up and see the monster inside him because he still sees that monster. I cup his face. "I believe you. I'm not going to wake up one day and hate you, Gabe. One day, I hope you'll wake up and say the same thing."

He lowers his forehead to mine, and for long seconds we sit there like that, but as it goes in this house, Dexter has doggy radar. He must be in the middle of all affectionate moments and soon he's nuzzling our laps and we're loving on him, smiling at each other. We're good. We're the best I've ever been.

Sunday morning, Gabe and I enjoy just being home together. We watch movies. We go for a run. We talk. We eat. We find creative ways to make love and it's wonderful. Even waking up Monday morning to reporters and news of Neal's confession to killing Kenneth doesn't mute the wonder of being here with Gabe and Dexter. Once we're at work, we set the craziness of the press aside, and I dive into learning my way around the office. Lulu is wonderful and it's clear we'll be friends. I even get to know Carrie, who also works for the company, actually owns part of the company as her family business merged with the Maxwells.

By Tuesday, the press is already dying down and word of the case closing finally arrives. There will be no interviews. It's over. Gabe and I celebrate with really hot sex and well-earned donuts. Later, at the office, life moves on. I embrace my new job by spending the morning at a conference table with Gabe, Carrie, and Reid talking through my role, creating their new philanthropy division. "We want you to present your ideas to us in a month," Reid announces. "And from those, we'll pick the best of the best, and you'll present those ideas, your ideas, to the board. That will be roughly two weeks later."

I perk up with a collision of nerves and adrenaline, but it's all positive. This is my chance to prove my worth. "What are my boundaries?" I ask.

Gabe slides a folder in front of me. "Your budget. The rest is up to you. You're the expert on non-profits."

I'm excited and Carrie shares my excitement. She feeds my eagerness to get started making my time here really count. We chat for a good hour after the men leave to attend to their clients. Carrie and I begin to bond and by the time I sit down behind my desk, alone in my thoughts, planning my presentations, I know that I'm on my way to a new life, a new way. This is not just Gabe's world. It's my world.

And hours later, when he steps inside my doorway, to check on me, I amend one part of that statement. This isn't his world and my world. This is our world.

That night we have dinner with Cat and Reese, celebrating the end of the investigation, as well as Reese winning the high-profile case he's been navigating through all of this. We do so with sparkling cider and baby talk, which does pinch a bit though I'd never admit that to anyone. Gabe and I will never have children. I have this thought, but quickly dismiss it. It doesn't matter. It really doesn't, but it does serve to remind me of his past, which is a painful one. I vow to wash away that pain and fill it will laughter. Not the fake laughter he'd used to hide his pain beneath but real, heartfelt laughter.

For the rest of the week, I'm eager to dive into my new job. With the shelter relocated, I analyze the best charitable way the company can contribute to society and what the tax-related credits will be, if any. I radiate toward filling the hole in the city that losing my mother's shelter has created.

Outside of work, Gabe and I spend every second together and fall into a routine. We workout together. We shower together. We sit in front of the fireplace and plan our future, the holidays. The travel we want to do together. The next weekend in the Hamptons, which I look forward to all week. We chopper in on Saturday morning.

Once we're there, we visit the shelter and my mother. I watch Gabe help a wounded dog come down off a fear-driven fit of aggression and fall in love with the man all over again.

"Animals know," my mother says beside me. "They hated Kenneth. They love Gabe. So, perhaps, should you."

"I do," I say softly. "I do, mother. I love him."

She brushes hair from my face. "And he loves you. I see it in his eyes."

There's barking and we both turn to find Gabe now playing run and fetch with yet another dog. "He needs a baby and not the furry kind," my mother suggests, winking at me, but thankfully moving on. "Though Gabbie and her babies are staying here. Brandon and I are too attached to let them go."

HER SUBMISSION

Brandon just happens to appear in that moment, sliding an arm around my mother's shoulders, and I know the look of love my mother described. I see it in Brandon's face when he looks at my mother. He's handsome and charming and as the day turns into a double dinner date, it becomes clear that he shares my mother's excitement for the shelter's future at his ranch. He's proud of her, as am I.

It's later that night, sitting by the outdoor fireplace, listening to the waves crash on the ocean that Gabe and I hatch the plan to open another shelter in the city, with my mother as the supervising veterinarian. We call her before we leave and invite her to breakfast. By the time we finish a breakfast that assures more jogging this week, we're all eager for a future new shelter in the city.

A month and a half flies by like it's mere hours, and I become less obsessed with keeping our relationship secret at the office, but vow to do so until after the board meeting where I will make my presentation. That day arrives, and I sit there with twelve hard expressions staring back at me. My presentation, which is completed with the aid of Dexter and Gabe, goes fabulously. Not only does the board approve of the shelter, quite a few members want to get involved. Dexter gives them high paws as appreciation. He also plays dead and dances. He's really good at convincing people he's not a serial killer. When the meeting is over, Gabe and Dexter kiss me in the lobby, and I don't care. I've made my claim on this life. I don't want to hide anymore.

The weekend arrives with Gabe's promise of a big surprise. "I'm taking you somewhere to celebrate your presentation. Dress up. We're going to do this right."

This pleases me and I have several days to settle on an emerald green dress with a flared skirt and cinched waist. Gabe dresses in a dark suit and wears a tie to match my dress. The restaurant is in a high-rise and I have no idea why, but there are butterflies in my belly as the waiter leads us to a private room just under an archway. There's a table set-up for us and champagne already on ice.

"This is amazing, Gabe," I say, claiming my seat as he holds it out for me, the view stunningly lit up with city lights doing their best at rivaling the starlight.

"As are you, Abbie." His voice softens. "As are you."

"Gabe," I whisper, emotion expanding in my chest.

He settles in the seat across from me and fills our glasses. We chat and sip our drinks when the waiter pokes his head inside and looks at Gabe. Gabe gives him a nod and then to my shock, Dexter walks in wearing a tie. I laugh as the pup offers me an envelope in his mouth. "What do you have there, boy?"

"Open it."

I unseal the flap and pull out what looks like pre-op paperwork. My brow furrows and I glance at Gabe. "What is this?"

"I'm getting a reversal. So I can be a father and you can be a mother, should we see fit. It's not a hundred percent, Abbie. I need you to know that, but—"

"Is this what you want? Really want?"

"I want everything with you, Abbie." And then he's on his knee beside me, holding out a velvet box. "Marry me. Marry me and make me the happiest man alive." He opens the lid and presents me with a glorious round diamond that glistens in the lights above. "You will never doubt my love."

Tears spill from my eyes. "Yes. Yes, of course I'll marry you." I press my hands to his face and my lips to his lips.

He stands and kisses me properly before sliding the ring on my finger. Dexter barks his approval and we promise him a steak for being such a handsome delivery boy. And I know that even if we don't get pregnant, we are already a perfect family.

THE END

Readers,

Thank you so much for picking up THE DIRTIER DUET! Gabe and Abbie's story touched my heart more than I could have imagined—Dexter, too!—and I hope they left a mark on you as well! What's next for me? I have **A PERFECT LIE**—my first thriller— coming out next month. Keep reading for chapter one! But also, join me for my sexy and suspenseful **NAKED TRILOGY** which will be debuting in June!

PRE-ORDER AND LEARN MORE HERE:

https://nakedtrilogy.weebly.com

In the mood for a cowboy romance? I have a brand-new one coming out this year in mass market paperback (in stores everywhere!) and ebook on August 27, 2019! Check it out here:

LISA RENEE JONES

https://www.goodreads.com/book/show/43582158-the-truth-about-cowboys

Don't forget, if you want to be the first to know about upcoming books, giveaways, sales and any other exciting news I have to share please be sure you're signed up for my newsletter! As an added bonus everyone receives a free ebook when they sign-up!

http://lisareneejones.com/newsletter-sign-up/

KEEP READING FOR CHAPTER ONE OF THE BASTARD (BOOK ONE IN MY SUPER SEXY FILTHY TRILOGY) AND A PERFECT LIE (MY UPCOMING PSYCHOLOGICAL THRILLER) !

THE FILTHY TRILOGY

BINGE THE ENTIRE SERIES NOW!

THE BASTARD (book one)
THE PRINCESS (book two)
THE EMPIRE (book three)

TURN THE PAGE TO READ CHAPTER ONE!

LISA RENEE JONES

CHAPTER ONE OF THE BASTARD

eric

When the Kingston family decides to throw a party, it means no less than two hundred people at their twenty-thousand-foot Aspen estate, valets at the door, an abundance of Kingston Motors luxury cars in the drive, and money. Lots of money, because Jeff Kingston has nothing to do with anyone who doesn't have money, aside from me, his bastard son, otherwise known as the backup heir just in case my half-brother kicks the bucket.

I exit the guest house, where I'm staying until my meeting with my father tomorrow, which I shouldn't have accepted. I don't know why the fuck I'm even here, aside from the fact that these people are supposed to be my people, and leaving the SEALs was like leaving family. It's hard to let go of that need for a family unit. Family. Right. What the hell was I thinking? Like I could ever really be a Kingston.

I walk down a stone path shrouded in flowers and low hanging trees, twisting left and then right until I enter the courtyard filled with bodies in fancy dresses and tuxedos like the one I'm in now. A waiter walks by and I snag a glass of champagne when I'd rather have whiskey, but I'll settle for anything to get me through tonight's launch of a new model of car. I barely give a shit about the old model, which is exactly why my father shouldn't want me to work for him. I walk to one of the few dozen standing tables covered in white tablecloths, down my drink and accept another when my gaze catches on a woman, on *her* and *just her*.

She's standing on the other side of the pool, a princess in a strappy black dress, with flawless skin and long brown hair, surrounded by her subjects. At least, that's how she reads to me, no doubt like every other socialite I've ever met in this godforsaken world, and yet I'm watching her when I never watch them. There's something about this woman, a white swan among the black swans on a pond made of money and death, my mother's death most specifically, since that's how I got here.

My princess must feel my attention because she tunes out the conversation she's having with several other people, her chin lifting, her gaze sweeping wide and then catching mine. I don't even think about looking away. I don't care that she knows that I'm watching her. I don't care if she knows that I'm thinking about fucking her. I'm the bastard in these parts. From the time I was thrust into this place right before my senior year of high school, I do what I do and everyone whispers about it. I'm not going to change that now. Let them whisper about what I want, and this woman, whoever the fuck she is, is worth the whispers.

The man next to her touches her elbow, his gaze shooting in my direction, his jaw setting hard with anger. Priceless and so typical of my father's class of people. He's pissed at me for getting his woman's attention. He should have fucked her better. My cellphone buzzes with a text message and I cut my stare, downing my champagne and then reaching for my phone to find a message from Grayson Bennett, a close friend from my first go at Harvard right before I left and went into the Navy. He's not a bastard, but rather the true heir to the Bennett empire.

Call me, his message says, which is typical Grayson. He wants something, he asks, and usually with actual words. And since we have unfinished business I don't want overheard, I walk toward the house where I know I can find that whiskey. I'll likely find the rightful heir to the throne, right along with our father as well, but at least I'll make my showing and get the hell out of here.

"There he is. My brother."

My jaw clenches at the sound of Isaac's voice even before he steps into my path, and as if for the first time ever he knows what I want, and cares, he offers me one of the two whiskey glasses in hand. "The good stuff. The kind we drink around these parts."

He doesn't mean we, as in me and him, he means we as in the Kingston family, which I've never been a part of. Our eyes lock and hold, the drama of the past, the hatred between us, and I have no doubt the crackle of energy around us is the attention of the room. We are after all the heir and would-be heir who hate each other. Him the prince, with thick, dark hair and green eyes, while I'm simply the bastard, with wavy brown hair, blue eyes, and a good four inches on Isaac at my height of six-foot-two. I don't look like I'm his blood. I damn sure don't feel like his blood, but my mother made sure I can't be denied. She took the damn DNA test that changed my life and not for the better in my opinion.

I accept the glass and his gaze goes to the ink peeking from beneath my white shirt, and lingers on the Rolex on my wrist, before lifting. "Looks like someone got all inked up."

"The bastard brother might as well look the role, right?"

"You're never going to let me live down calling you that, now are you?"

"You don't need to live it down, Isaac, but you will have to face me every day if I decide to join the company, and we both know that didn't go well for you at Harvard."

His eyes spark with a familiar anger I don't have to intentionally stir. He hates me for being the bastard child of his father's mistress, the brother thrust on him only months after his mother died. An ironic turn of events considering my mother's cancer. He steps closer, toe to toe, all up close and friendly. "If you think that because you're some sort of SEAL Team Six hero or something, that I won't buckle you right at the knees, you're wrong. You will not take what is mine."

"I see you two got right back into the brotherly love."

At the sound of my father's voice, Isaac grimaces and my lips quirk. "Seems we have," I say, as Isaac rotates and we both face my father, who looks fit and younger than his fifty-four years in his tuxedo with his dark hair. "I have someone I want you to meet," he says, and The Princess steps to his side, her crystal blue eyes meeting mine as my father says, "Eric. Meet your stepsister, Harper."

LEARN MORE HERE:

http://filthytrilogy.lisareneejones.com

A PERFECT LIE

A brand-new psychological thriller coming May 14, 2019!

They say that you are not a product of the environment that you've grown up in, that you create your own story, tell it your way. That you get to pick your own future. They lied. If you're honest with yourself, you believed that lie, too, like I used to, because I wanted to, and even needed to believe that I had some semblance of control over my own self. The truth is that control is part of the lie. The ability to become a person of our own making is the perfect lie. I concede that it might appear that some people control their destiny, but I assure you, if you gave me fifteen minutes, I could pull apart that façade. We are born into a destiny that we never have the chance to escape. That's why I must tell my story. For those of you out there like me who were told that you have choices, when you never had one single choice that was your own. For those of you out there who were, who are, judged for decisions you've made that were directed by your destiny, not by the façade of choices. The irony of the story within this story is how one person's predisposed destiny can impact, influence, and even change the lives of those around him or her. How one destiny ties to another destiny.

I am Hailey Anne Monroe. I'm twenty-eight years old. An artist, who found her muse on the canvas because I wasn't allowed to have friends or even keep a journal. And yes, if you haven't guessed by now, I'm that Hailey Anne Monroe, daughter to Thomas Frank Monroe, the man who was a half-percentage point from becoming President of the United States. If you were able to ask him, he'd probably tell you that I was the half point. But you can't ask him, and he can't tell you. He's dead. They're all dead and now I can speak.

TURN THE PAGE TO READ CHAPTER ONE!

CHAPTER ONE OF A PERFECT LIE

hailey anne monroe

You already know that I'm one of those perfect lies we've discussed, a façade of choices that were never my own. But that one perfect lie is too simplistic to describe who, and what, I am. I am perhaps a dozen perfect lies, the creation of at least one of those lies beginning the day I was born. That's when the clock started ticking. That's when decisions started being made for me. That's when every step that could be taken was to ensure I was "perfect." My mother, a brilliant doctor, ensured I was one hundred percent healthy, in all ways a test, pin prick, and inspection could ensure. I was, of course, vaccinated on a strict schedule, because in my household we must be so squeaky clean that we cannot possibly give anything to anyone.

Meanwhile, my father, the consummate politician, began planning my college years while my diapers were still being changed. I would be an attorney. I would go to an Ivy League college. I would be a part of the elite. Therefore, I was with tutors before I could spell. I was in dance at five years old. Of course, there was also piano, and French, Spanish, and Chinese language classes. The one joy I found was in an art class, which my mother suggested when I was twelve. It became my obsession, my one salvation, my one escape.

Outside of her. She was not like my father. She was my friend, not my dictator. She was the bridge between us. The one we both adored. She listened to me. She listened to him. She tried to find compromise between us. She gave me choices, within the limits I was allowed. She tried to make me happy. She did make me as happy as anyone who was a puppet to a political machine could be, but the bigger the machine, the more developed, the harder that became. And still she fought for me.

I loved my mother with all of my heart and soul.

That's why it's hard to tell this part of my story. If there was one moment, beyond my birth, that established my destiny, and my influence on the destiny of those around me, it would be one evening during my senior year in high school, the night I killed my mother.

The past—twelve years ago...

The steps leading to the Michaels' home seem to stretch eternally, but then so do most on this particular strip of houses in McLean, Virginia, where the rich, and sometimes famous, reside. Music radiates from the walls of the massive white mansion that is our destination, the stretch of land owned by the family wide enough that the nearest neighbor sees nothing and hears nothing. They most certainly don't know that while the Michaels are out of town, their son, Jesse, is throwing a party.

"I can't believe we're at Jesse's house," Danielle says, linking her arm through mine, something she's been doing for the past six years, since we met in private school at age eleven. Only then I was the tall one, and now I'm five-foot-four to her five-foot-eight, and that's when I'm wearing heels and she's not.

"Considering his father bloodies my father on his news program nightly, I can't either," I say. "I shouldn't be here, Danielle."

She stops walking and turns to me, her beautiful chestnut hair, which goes with her beautiful, perfect face and body, blowing right smack into my average face. She shoves said beautiful hair behind her ears, and glowers at me. "Hailey—"

"Don't start," I say, folding my arms in front of my chest, which is at least respectable, considering my dirty blonde hair and blue eyes are what I call average and others call cute. Like I'm not smart enough to know that means average. "I'm here. You already got me here."

"Jesse doesn't care about your father's run for President," she argues. "Or that his father doesn't support your father."

"Why did you just say that?" I demand.

"Say what?"

"Now you've just reminded me that I'm at the house of a man who doesn't support my father, whom I happen to love. I need to leave." I start down the stairs.

Danielle hops in front of me. "Wait. Please. I think I might be in love with Jesse. You can't just leave."

"My God, woman, you're a drama queen. You have never even kissed him. And I have to study for the SAT and so do you."

"Please. His father isn't here. His father will never know about the party or us."

"Danielle, if my father finds out—"

"He's out of town, too. How is he going to find out?"

"What about your father? He's an advisor to my father. You can't date Jesse."

She draws in a deep breath, her expression tightening before she gushes out, *"Hailey,"* making my name a plea. "I'm trying so hard to be normal. I know that you deal with things by studying. I do, but I need this. I need to feel normal."

Normal.

That word punches me with a fist of emotions I reject every time I hear it and feel them. "We will never be normal again and you know it. We weren't normal to start with. Not when—"

"After that night," she says. "We were normal enough until then. But since—after what happened, after we—"

"Stop," I hiss. "We don't talk about it. We don't talk about it *ever*."

"Ouch," she says, grabbing my hand that is on her arm, my grip anything but gentle. "You're hurting me."

I have to count to three and force myself to breathe again before my fingers ease from her arm. "We agreed that 'the incident' was buried."

"Right," she says, and now she's hugging herself. "Because we're so good at burying things."

"We have to be," I bite out, trying to soften my tone and failing. "I *know* you know that."

She gives me several choppy nods. "Yes." Her voice is tiny. "I know." She turns pragmatic, her tone lifting. "I just need more to clutter up my mind than the SAT exam. That will come and go."

"And then there will be more work ahead."

"I need more," she insists. "I need to be normal."

"You will never—"

"I can pretend, okay? I need to *feel* normal even if I'm not. And even if you don't admit it, so do you."

My fingers curl, my nails cutting into my palms, perhaps because she's right. Some part of me cared when I put on my best black jeans and a V-neck black sweater that shows my assets. Some part of me wanted to look as good as she does in her pink lacy off-the-shoulder blouse and faded jeans. Some part of me forgot that the "normal" ship sailed for me the day I was born to a father who aspired to be President, but still, I don't disagree with her. I need to get her head on straight and maybe kissing Jesse is exactly the distraction that she needs do the trick. I link my arm with hers once more. "Let's go see Jesse."

She gives me one of her big smiles and I know that I've made the right decision, because when she's smiling like that no one sees anything but beauty which is exactly how it needs to stay. And so, I make that walk with her up those steps, climbing toward what I hope is not a bad decision, when I swore I was done with those. Nevertheless, in a matter of two minutes, we're on the giant concrete porch, a Selena Gomez song radiating from the walls and rattling my teeth.

The door flies open, and several kids I've seen around, but don't know, stagger outside while Danielle pulls me into the gaudy glamour of the Michaels' home, which is as far opposite of my conservative father as the talk show host's politics. The floors are white and gray marble. The furniture is boxy and flat, with red and orange accents, with the added flair of newly added bottles, bags, cups, and people. There are lots of people everywhere, including on top of the grand piano. It's like my high school class, inclusive of the football team and cheerleaders, has been dropped inside a bad Vegas hotel room. Or so I've heard and seen in movies. I've not actually been to Vegas; that would be far too scandalous for a future first daughter, or so says my father.

"Where now?" I ask, leaning into Danielle.

"He said the backyard," she replies, scanning. "This way!" she adds, and suddenly she's dragging me through several groups of about a half-dozen bodies.

Our destination is apparently the outdoor patio, where a fire is burning in a stone pit, and despite it being April, and in the sixties, surrounded by a cluster of ottoman-like seating and lanterns on steel poles. Plus, more people are here, and now instead of Selena Gomez rattling my teeth, it's Rihanna.

"Danielle!" The shout comes from Jesse, who is sitting in a cluster of people to our far left. Of course, Danielle starts dragging me forward again, which has me feeling like her cute dog that doesn't want to be walked. Correction: Her forgotten dog that doesn't want to be walked, considering she lets go of me and runs to Jesse, giving him a big hug. I'm left with one open seat, smack between two football players: David Nelson and Ramon Miller. Both are hot. Both have dark hair, though Ramon's is curly and excessive, and David's is buzzed, understandably since I think I heard his dad is military. Okay, I know his dad is military because I've been crushing on him since he showed up at school six months ago.

I sit awkwardly between them, and stare desperately at Danielle, who just stuck her tongue down Jesse's throat in a familiar way that says it's not the first time. *I need to leave*, I think. I'll just get up and leave, but then, what if she panics? What if she forgets that Jesse can't be in on 'the incident'? We can never tell anyone what happened. Why did I think this night was a good distraction?

"Hey there," David says, piercing me with his blue eyes.

"Hi," I say.

"You look like you want to crawl under a rock," he comments.

"Do you know where I can find one?"

He laughs. He has a good laugh. A genuine laugh and since I don't know many people who do anything genuinely, I feel that hard spot in my belly begin to soften. "I'll help you find one if you take me with you."

"You don't belong under a rock," I say.

He arches a brow. "And you do?"

"Belong," I say. "No. But happier there right now, yes."

"That hurts my feelings," he says, holding his hand to his chest as if wounded.

"Oh. No. Sorry. I just meant…I don't do parties."

"Because your dad is a politician," he assumes.

"He doesn't exactly approve of events like this."

He laughs again. "Events. Right." His hand settles on my leg and there is this funny sensation in my belly. "I'll make sure nothing goes wrong. Okay?"

"No. No, I'll make sure nothing goes wrong."

He leans in and presses his cheek to mine, his lips by my ear. "Then I'll give you extra protection." I inhale, and he pulls back, suddenly no longer touching me.

My gaze lifts and I find Danielle looking at me with a big grin on her face. David hands me a shot glass and Jesse hands Danielle one. She nods, and I don't know why, but I just do it. I down the liquid in what is my first drink ever. The next thing I know, David's tongue is down my throat and when I blink, I'm not even sitting on the back patio anymore. I'm lying on a bed and he's pulling his shirt off. And I don't know how I got here. I don't know what is happening. Panic rises with a sense of being out of control. I stand up and David reaches for me, but I shove at him.

"No!"

I dart around him and I must be drunk but I think my feet are too steady to be drunk. I run from the room and keep running down a hallway and to the stairs. I grab the railing, flashes of images in my mind. David offering me another drink. Me refusing. David kissing me and offering me yet another drink. I had refused. So why was I just on a bed and unaware of how I got there?

"Hailey!"

At the sound of David's voice, I take off down the steps, not even sure where I'm going, but I don't stop. I push through bodies and I'm on the porch in what feels like slow motion. I'm running down the stairs. I'm leaving. I have to get out of here.

I blink awake, cold, with a hard surface at my back. Gasping with the shock of disorientation, I sit up, the first orange and red of a new day in the darkness of the sky. I'm outside. I'm…I look around and realize that I'm on the bench of a picnic table. I'm in a park. I stand up and start to pace. I'm dressed in black jeans and a black sweater. The party. I went to the party. I dig my heels in. Did I get drunk? Wouldn't I feel sick? I'm not sick. I'm not unsteady. My tiny purse I carry with me often is at my hip. I unzip it and pull out my phone. Ten calls from my mother. No messages from Danielle.

"Danielle," I whisper. "Where is Danielle?"

I dial her number and she doesn't answer. I dial again. And again. I press my hand to my face and look at the time. Five in the morning. My car is at Jesse's house. I start walking, looking for a sign, anything to tell me where I'm at. Finally, I find a sign: *Rock Creek Park.* The party was in McLean. Rock Creek is back in Washington, a good forty minutes away. I lean against the sign and my mother calls again.

I answer. "Mom?"

"Thank God," she breathes out, her voice filled with both panic and anger, two things that my mother, a gentle soul, and doctor, who loves people, rarely allows to surface. "Oh, thank God. I've been so worried."

"I don't know what happened, Mom. I blacked out and I'm at a park."

"Near Rock Creek," she says. "I know. I did the 'find my phone' search but it's not exact and I was about to call the police. I just knew—" She sobs before adding, "I just knew you were dead in the woods. I was about to get help. I was about to have a search start."

"I—Mom, I—"

"Go to the main parking lot." She hangs up.

My cellphone rings with Danielle's number. "Where are you?" I demand.

"At Jesse's," she says. "Where are you? I was asleep and I thought you were in a room with David, but he was with some other girl."

"You don't know what happened to me?" I ask.

"No. Jesus. What happened?"

Headlights shine in my direction from a parking lot. "I'll call you later," I say. "I have to deal with my mother." I hang up and start running toward the lights. By the time I'm at the driver's side of my mother's Mercedes, she's there, too, out of the car and reaching for me.

"You have so much to explain," she attacks, grabbing my arms and hugging me. "I am furious with you. You scared me."

"I scared me, too," I say hugging her, starting to cry, the scent of her jasmine perfume, consuming my senses, and calming me. "I don't know what happened."

She pulls back. "Did you drink and do drugs?"

"No. I mean—one drink. I'm fine. I—"

"One drink. We both know what that means. This wasn't the first time."

"No. Mom. It was. One drink. I don't know what happened. Someone drugged me. They had to have drugged me."

Her lips purse. "Get in the car."

"Mom—"

"Get in the car."

I nod and do as I'm told. I get in the car. The minute she's in with me, I try to explain. "Mom, I—"

"Do not speak to me until I calm down." He seatbelt warning beeps.

"Mom—"

"Shut up, Hailey," she says, putting us in motion.

I suck in air at the harsh words that do not fit my mother, who is not just beautiful, but graceful in her actions and words. Perfect, actually, and everything I aspire to be. I click my belt while her warning continues to go off. She turns us onto the highway and I listen to the warning going off, trying to fill the blank space in my head with answers I can give her. But there are none and suddenly she lets out a choked sound and hits the brakes. My eyes jolt open, but everything is spinning. We're spinning. I can't see or move. "Mom!" I shout, I think. Or maybe I don't. Glass shatters. I feel it on my face, cutting me, digging into my skin.

We jolt again, no longer spinning, but the world goes black.

Time is still.

And then there are sirens and I try to catch my breath, but my chest hurts so badly. "Mom," I whisper, turning to look at her but she's not there. She's not there. Panic rises fast and hard and I unhook my belt and ball my fist at my aching chest. Forcing myself to move, I sit up to find my mother on the hood of the car, a huge chunk of steel through her body.

I scream and I can't stop screaming. I can't stop screaming.

PRE-ORDER A PERFECT LIE HERE:

https://aperfectliebook.weebly.com

WANT MORE LISA RENEE JONES ROMANCE?

Have you read my Dirty Rich series? A series of super sexy lawyers filled with passion and mystery! Check it out here:

http://dirtyrich.lisareneejones.com

NEW STANDALONE COMING IN MY LILAH LOVE SERIES!

This series is a suspense series with a steamy side of romance! The first two books are available now, but the third book can be read as a standalone as well!

https://www.lilahlove.com/

ALSO BY LISA RENEE JONES

THE INSIDE OUT SERIES

If I Were You
Being Me
Revealing Us
*His Secrets**
Rebecca's Lost Journals
*The Master Undone**
*My Hunger**
No In Between
*My Control**
I Belong to You
*All of Me**

THE SECRET LIFE OF AMY BENSEN

Escaping Reality
Infinite Possibilities
Forsaken
*Unbroken**

CARELESS WHISPERS

Denial
Demand
Surrender

WHITE LIES

Provocative
Shameless

TALL, DARK & DEADLY

Hot Secrets
Dangerous Secrets
Beneath the Secrets

WALKER SECURITY

Deep Under
Pulled Under
Falling Under

LILAH LOVE

Murder Notes
Murder Girl
Love Me Dead (2019)
Love Kills (2019)

DIRTY RICH

Dirty Rich One Night Stand
Dirty Rich Cinderella Story
Dirty Rich Obsession
Dirty Rich Betrayal
Dirty Rich Cinderella Story: Ever After
Dirty Rich One Night Stand: Two Years Later
Dirty Rich Obsession: All Mine

THE FILTHY TRILOGY

The Bastard
The Princess
The Empire

THE NAKED TRILOGY

One Man (June 2019)
One Woman (September 2019)
Two Together (November 2019)

*eBook only

ABOUT THE AUTHOR

New York Times and USA Today bestselling author Lisa Renee Jones is the author of the highly acclaimed INSIDE OUT series.

In addition to the success of Lisa's INSIDE OUT series, she has published many successful titles. The TALL, DARK AND DEADLY series and THE SECRET LIFE OF AMY BENSEN series, both spent several months on a combination of the New York Times and USA Today bestselling lists. Lisa is also the author of the bestselling LILAH LOVE and WHITE LIES series.

Prior to publishing, Lisa owned multi-state staffing agency that was recognized many times by The Austin Business Journal and also praised by the Dallas Women's Magazine. In 1998 Lisa was listed as the #7 growing women owned business in Entrepreneur Magazine.

Lisa loves to hear from her readers. You can reach her on Twitter and Facebook daily.

Printed in Great Britain
by Amazon